IN THE

Jacob shook his head. "Not ghosts—a *witch*. Long time ago there was a colonial settlement here. For a while, the people almost didn't survive. Droughts, blight, and long cold winters killed over half the settlers in the village. Your house stands on a spot where an old woman used to live alone, and they accused her of witchcraft. They suspected her of casting spells over the village and burying the bodies of her enemies under her cabin. They burned her house down and ran her out of the settlement. But she swore she'd be back for her vengeance, and it would cost the lives of three local children. Their blood would make her young and powerful...and immortal."

... LURKS HORROR

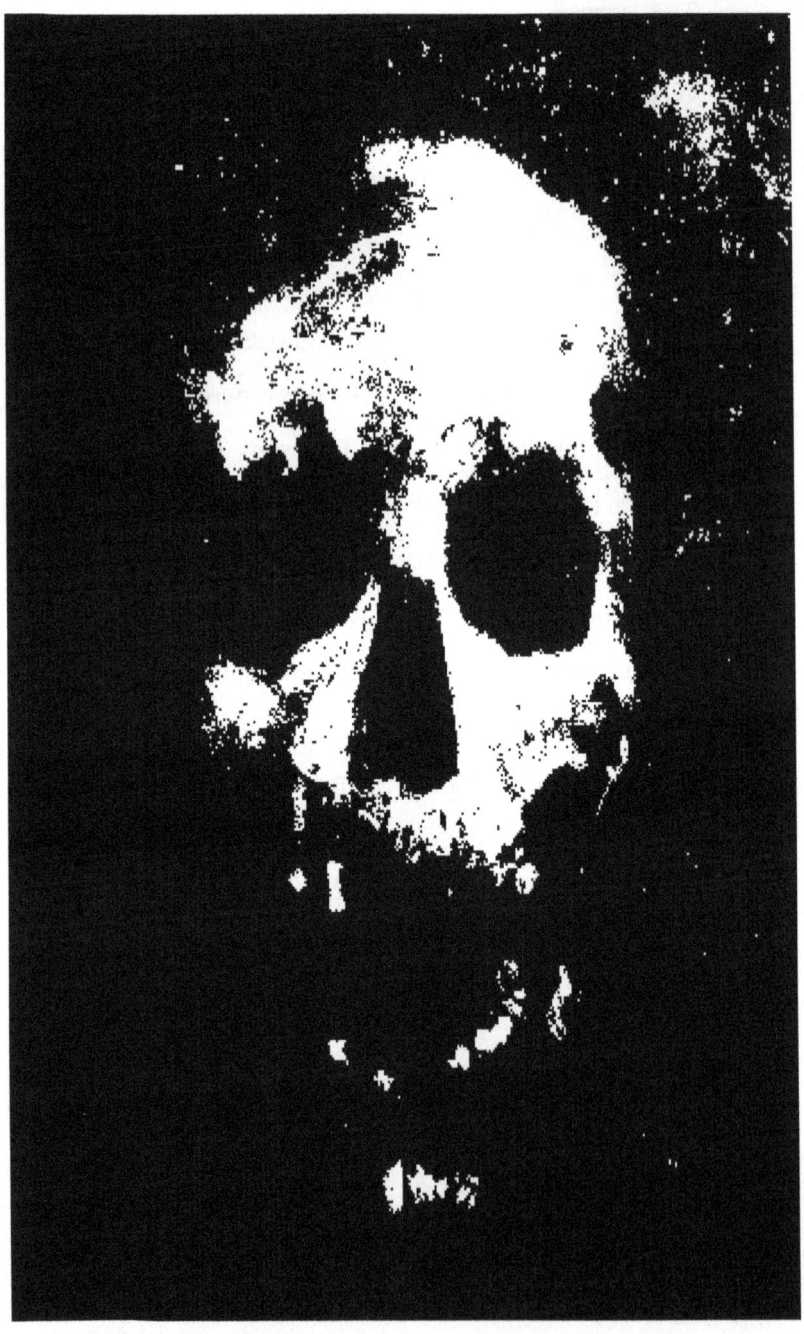

THE DEAD OF NIGHT

10 TALES OF TERROR

David R. Smith

with Olivia Ann Smith

DARK DREAMS PUBLICATIONS

This is a work of fiction. Names, characters, places and incidents are the products of the author's imagination or are used fictitiously, and any resemblance to actual persons, living or dead, business establishments, events or locales, is entirely coincidental.

Copyright © 2020 by David R. Smith
All rights reserved. No part of this book may be reproduced without permission from the author, David R. Smith, excepting for brief passages appearing in a review for a newspaper or magazine.

ISBN: 978-0-578-783314

For ordering information, contact the author at drsmithbooks@gmail.com or visit www.davidrsmithbooks.com

Printed in the United States of America

Book cover designed by Jennifer Hamson

For Alex
-D.R.S.

For Grandma Smith
-O.A.S.

**Other Horror Books by
David R. Smith**

Curse of the Witch
The Halloween House
The Edge of Midnight
Darkness Falling
The Door to Andara
Let 'Em Rip: 13 Tales of Horror

Coming in 2021
Locker 200

ACKNOWLEDGMENTS

Many people help in the creation of a new book. A special debt of gratitude is owed to my wife, Jennifer, for being the first reader of all my manuscripts. She sees them in their rawest form and doesn't even flinch. Thank you to Sarah Goodman-Brown for helping to find those little mistakes that like to hide from their creator and torment him. And to Michael Sisson for his exceptionally close reading and editing, ensuring this book is polished and ready for prime time. As always, a tip of the hat to Jennifer Hamson for her eerie cover art. If you judge this book favorably by its cover, you know who to thank.

Contents

Introduction	1
Masks	8
Running the Road	22
The Trapdoor	44
The Incident	72
The Light House	92
I'll Return for You	122
Leeches	136
One Winter Night	152
The Midnight Chariot	158
The Root of All Evil	170

INTRODUCTION

"Alone. Yes, that's the key word, the most awful word in the English tongue. Murder doesn't hold a candle to it and hell is only a poor synonym."
— Stephen King

Where I grew up, about a quarter of a mile from a shopping mall and a busy interstate highway, the nighttime hours were anything but silent. Long-haul truckers' noisy rigs would go blasting through the neighborhood. And the constant shushing of cars speeding along the interstate was a nuisance if you were trying to enjoy a peaceful evening.

Some nights the noise pollution was so bad, I would close all the doors and windows so I could hear the TV. I didn't care if it was stifling hot; I just couldn't stand the *noise* anymore.

Since then I've moved to a more pastoral setting in a small town. Not too far off the beaten track, but far enough away from busy highways and byways that at night I can hear…nothing.

The sound of nothing is anything but silent. I can stand in my backyard and detect the faintest of breezes in the trees overhead. I can hear the rustle of an animal foraging nearby, or the faint yet plaintive howl of a lonely dog prowling the neighborhood.

And sometimes I don't hear any of those things at all. Instead I hear …

Footsteps pacing on a creaky floor.

The click of a claw on stone pavement.

A snort or threatening growl.

In other words, solitude stirs a writer's senses. Our mind's eye sees without distraction what is waiting over the next horizon.

And let it not go unnoticed that the world has a way of springing its deepest, darkest nightmares on us at our most vulnerable moments. When we're alone.

In the dead of night.

Each of these stories presents a unique take on loneliness, where terror seeps up silently around our feet, ready to swallow us whole. Where nothing is as it seems. Maybe it's an unearthly scream in the middle of the night. A black mist conjured by a voodoo ritual ready to steal your soul. Or justice served from beyond the grave.

For an added treat, my daughter Olivia has co-authored two stories in this collection. Be careful when you look through the trapdoor of her imagination. You may not like what surprises wait for you in the dark.

Whatever the horror—whatever you *think* you hear or see in the dark—let me remind you there is always something far, far worse to be feared. Something coiled like a loathsome insect in the cellar of your imagination, gazing out at you from its hidey-hole. Watching you. Making sure you're alone.

Enjoy the peace and quiet while you can.

It won't last long.

"I think perhaps all of us go a little crazy at times."
— Robert Bloch, *Psycho*

"Imagination, of course, can open any door - turn the key and let terror walk right in."
— Truman Capote

When you were here before
Couldn't look you in the eye
You're just like an angel
Your skin makes me cry
— Radiohead, *Creep*

MASKS

Heavy rain thudded the windows of the downtown office building of Mann & Associates as the woman worked feverishly to catch up on paperwork.

According to the wall clock, midnight had come and gone. By now the building would be empty, but she stayed behind as always, collecting overtime as if the practice were going out of style.

Erin glanced up from her computer screen and found herself staring directly into the hollow eyes of a pumpkin. The dying orange-red candle flame flickered lightly in a passing breeze.

Just another stupid holiday, she thought.

The pumpkin's grin seemed to grow wider.

"I'll never understand people's obsessions with costumes and candy and trick-or-treat. Or you." She looked away from the pumpkin.

The candle flame guttered and went out.

The room grew darker. Shadows appeared in all corners of her cramped little office. Or was it her imagination? In any case, she was exhausted. Erin rubbed her eyes and stood up from her desk. A sudden longing for sleep came over her. She grabbed her coat and purse and headed for the door.

"Good night, Jack," she said to the pumpkin as she turned off the lights.

The long hall in front of her was deserted and silent, with red emergency exit signs the only source of light. Her footsteps reverberated all around her, as if somebody else were walking right beside her. She reached the elevator shaft and pushed the button for a car, waiting anxiously. She felt smothered by the darkness and vast emptiness of the building, like being trapped in an underwater cave with the tide rolling in.

She pushed the elevator button again impatiently. When at last the doors wheezed open, she stepped back in shock. A man in dirty blue cover-alls stood in the middle of the car, hands clasped calmly before him, a rumpled white shopping bag on the floor by his feet. He was medium build, standing close to six feet tall. His eyes, almost the same muddy brown as his hair, stared blankly straight ahead before he noticed her stunned appearance.

"Oh, good evening. I hope I didn't startle you." A smile spread across his lips. "I guess I was working the late shift like you."

Despite his unkempt appearance, the man's quiet voice was pleasant enough, with an unusual foreign accent she couldn't place.

The man reached out to hold the elevator doors open. "Are you coming on?" he asked. "Or are you waiting for the next one?" He smiled even wider, revealing a mouth crowded with large white teeth.

She felt foolish standing there so uncertainly. *I should wait for the next one*, she thought. But the thought of hanging around here any longer prompted her to step into the elevator. Besides, ten floors weren't that many. How long would it take to descend…twenty seconds? Thirty, at most?

"Lobby, please," she said, avoiding his eyes.

"I figured you weren't going to the roof." The man pressed the Lobby button and then took a step back. Erin felt his eyes bore into the nape of her neck, an unpleasant feeling like tiny insects burrowing under her skin. She suddenly questioned herself for getting into the elevator. At any moment she expected him to pull out a knife or grab her by the throat and start viciously strangling her.

Didn't it always happen that way in the horror movies? A naïve female, unwilling to trust her own instincts, finds herself cornered in a dark place by a criminally insane man who looks, for all intents and purposes, like a normal guy?

Except, of course, he was a rampaging murderer. Was that how this was going to end?

Slowly, she slid one step to the right, putting a little room between herself and the stranger. In case she needed to escape. *But where are you going to go, Erin? You've trapped yourself in here with him!* After what seemed like an eternity, the elevator doors squeezed shut and the car began to move.

"I'm Merrick," the man said in a voice barely above a whisper.

"Erin," she answered him, hoping that would be the extent of their pleasantries. It wasn't.

"I know," he said. "Everyone else went home hours ago to celebrate Halloween. Why are you still here?"

9...8...

"Because it's still a business day. I like working late."

7...6...

"Halloween is one of our most ancient customs. The Druids believed it was the night when the dead sought the living. Where's your holiday spirit? Where's your *enthusiasm*?"

5…4…

"My enthusiasm's for money," she said. "That corner office up there? Someday that's going to be *mine*. I've been working my butt off to get promoted to Vice President of International Sales."

"Sounds impressive."

3…2…

"It is."

1…

The elevator crashed to a halt. Erin was flung to the floor with brutal force. The vibration of grinding gears and a violent rattling rocked the compartment. Her head spun, and pain shot wildly through her back. When the rattling ceased and silence returned, Erin had a moment of realization that more than the elevator's mechanism had been shattered in that moment.

She was trapped, with a man she did not know, who'd had his eye on her from the beginning.

She fought back panic with an iron will as she stood on rubbery legs and gathered her wits. Above her, the lights blinked between first floor and lobby.

"Are you all right?" Merrick asked, sounding worried.

"I'm fine," she replied curtly.

"Let me help you—" He tried to support her around her lower back, but she brushed his arm away.

"I said *I'm fine.*" She knew how she sounded but didn't care. She prided herself on her fierce independence, a single woman who took no crap from anyone. She wasn't about to change that now.

Smoothing out her clothes, Erin pushed the button for the lobby, hoping it would work. The effort, of course, was useless.

Next, she took out her cell phone and tried to make a call—but within this steel cage there were no bars to be found.

She leaned against the wall and sighed.

"We might be stuck here all night," Merrick said.

"Don't get too excited," Erin snapped. "They'll get us out soon."

"'They'? Who do you think is coming? It's after midnight."

Erin didn't answer. But then a thought occurred to her.

"Hey, you're like a maintenance man or something, right?"

"Something like that."

"Could you fix this thing?"

Merrick looked up at the glowing ceiling panels. Puzzlement crossed his face before he said, "No, not from in here. Besides, I don't have my tools with me."

Erin's gaze dropped to the floor. "Then what's in the bag?"

He slid the bag away from her with his foot. "Nothing. Just…a mask."

"A mask?" she repeated, catching herself before she could laugh. "Can I see it? Put it on!"

Just then she felt the terror of the potentially dangerous situation she was in start to ebb away.

Merrick now seemed less of a threat to harm her and more like an overgrown goofy kid on his way to an adolescent masquerade party. *Where they probably still dunk for apples, and, when Mom's not looking, spike the punch.*

"I don't think you'll like it very much," Merrick demurred, looking away from her.

She felt the roles reversing now as she took a step toward him and he edged away from her. "Try me."

"I thought you didn't have any Halloween spirit."

I don't, she thought. *But teasing weirdos like you always lifts my spirits.*

In that moment he reminded Erin of her ex-husband Mitch. The contempt she felt every time she came home from another grueling day at the office to find him sitting on the couch reading one of his stupid science fiction novels. Busting her ass all day to pay the bills while he sat around collecting unemployment checks because he couldn't sell any of his novel manuscripts to publishers.

The disdain grew until she finally decided to leave him. He was a blithering mess that day, weeping like a baby when she packed the SUV and drove off, but no one could claim she wasn't decent toward him at the end. She let him keep the house and kids, which wasn't a big loss to her; their two sons were just as shiftless as their father.

After a few seconds, his expression changed from resolve to surrender. He reached down into the bag and pulled out a grotesque mask. Hair stuck out in snarled clumps all over the spiny head. The mouth, deformed and ringed in what looked like dried blood, was horribly twisted and frozen in a snarl. Two rows of rubber fangs designed to look like rotted teeth poked out of the pinkish gums.

Without warning, Merrick slipped the mask on over his head. Immediately his breathing became raspy and labored, as though he were suffocating inside it. His eyes gleamed through the mask, full of a hunger that hadn't been there a moment ago. A hunger for *her*. Erin instantly regretted asking to see the mask. The monstrous design of it sickened her, and a stale smell of sweat and the coppery tang of blood filled the elevator compartment. Her stomach threatened to spew her dinner all over the floor.

"Take it off," she said, waving him away as he inched toward her. "It's revolting and its smells."

"I don't smell anything," he replied in a voice deep and guttural like an animal's. "Except your fear."

"That's very funny. Take off the mask."

"You first."

"What are you talking about?"

Merrick loomed over her. "I've watched you for months now, scurrying around this place like a rat in a maze, ignorant of everything and everybody except your job. I say good morning to you every single day, but you never say it back, so focused are you on your schemes. You're the sort who lives her whole life in service to money, with self-promotion as your only interest. You're the worst kind of person—"

"Screw you."

"—in a world full of terrible people. So self-absorbed you don't feel or even acknowledge the suffering of others."

"Are you suffering? Is that it, Merrick? Maybe cleaning toilets isn't paying the rent, eh?"

"You look but you do not see," Merrick's eyes grew distant and his words soft-spoken yet clear: 'You are those who justify yourselves before men, but God knows your hearts. For what is exalted among men is an abomination in the sight of God.'"

That quote. She remembered it from Catholic school.

"This is about our recent acquisition, isn't it?" she said in a shaky voice. "Look, we gave those people severance checks…"

"No, it isn't about any one thing. It's the pattern of your life, Erin. You are all tricks and no *treats*."

Erin scoffed. "Ridiculous."

Merrick reached out for her, but she slapped his hand away, shrinking into the corner.

"Stop it. You're scaring me."

"Not as much as you scare me."

"Take off that mask!" she pleaded.

"You don't understand, do you?" He reached up and felt the mask, running his hands through the tufts of hair and along the sides of its mouth, massaging the elastic skin. "I'm not wearing one. This is who I am."

Erin screamed.

"But you seem to be having difficulty with yours." Merrick slid a long, serrated knife out of the pocket of his cover-alls. "Here, let me help you remove it..."

RUNNING THE ROAD

The screaming of metal and the shattering of glass startled Daniel out of a deep sleep.

He sat bolt upright, soiled newspapers crinkling and fluttering about him. A woman's shrill cry for help echoed across the concrete jungle of the city. Daniel climbed groggily out of his filthy Whirlpool box, wincing at the pain in his knees, and clutching at his stomach.

Last night's dinner was moldy egg rolls, found at the bottom of a Chinese restaurant's dumpster, and they weren't sitting too well. He wished he could have gone inside to eat but he couldn't, not dressed like this, in tattered, grungy clothes stuck to his sweaty body like paste. He wouldn't dare.

Mr. Daniel P. Simmons, at one time a promising young investment banker on Wall Street, had the craggy face of a man twice his age. His eyes, once a sharp and penetrating blue, sunk deep into the black chasms of his wasted skull. His teeth were chipped and stained yellow, and most days they ached terribly. His scruffy cheeks sported two weeks of beard since the last time he scraped it off with a used razor he'd found in a gutter. His hair hung down to the nape of his neck in tangled, oily strands. Sometimes when he looked at himself in the mirror, he barely recognized himself anymore.

What have I become?

This time a man's voice cried out for help, jolting him out of his reverie. Daniel shuffled out into the street. There was no traffic yet at this early Sunday morning hour; the movers and shakers were no doubt still in bed sleeping off last night's revelry. All was calm and peaceful, except for the smoking wreckage of a small car that had wrestled with a utility pole and lost. It sat like a squashed bug, shards of glass glittering on the street like snowflakes. A slow *drip, drip* of blood oozed out of the passenger side door. From this distance of about fifty feet away, Daniel could make out two bodies, one being a woman's, moaning and coughing; the other a man's, slouched over the steering wheel, looking about dazedly.

Daniel approached warily, glancing furtively over his shoulder, afraid he might get caught and blamed somehow for the accident. But except for the injured couple and the slight hiss of steam escaping the car's engine, the street was quiet, and he was quite alone.

That's no cheap sedan, he noticed as he drew closer. It was a Porsche. Daniel used to know a guy who owned one. A coffin on wheels, he used to joke, to his friend's displeasure. Daniel preferred his Cadillac Escalade. He always felt protected in that big gas-guzzling tank, insulated from the unpredictability of other drivers.

Daniel peered through the passenger's smashed side window and found the woman gasping for breath, a shard of glass sticking out of her thigh. The man in the driver's seat groaned, his eyes fluttering. A gaping wound in his chest gushed blood. The swampy reek of alcohol wafted on their breaths. Both the woman and man were dressed elegantly, apparently returning from some fancy gala. Daniel remembered those days, the parties on the Upper West Side, his beautiful wife…

"Help us," the woman gasped. "Call…for…an ambulance."

Daniel didn't know what to do. He had no cell phone of course, and the nearest apartment building was two blocks away. Besides, who would open the door to a stranger in the middle of the night?

The driver shifted his weight slightly. And that's when Daniel saw it, a glint of something oddly bright and metallic. His breath caught in his throat.

This man, whoever he was—and he must have been somebody special—had a most unusual hand. It shined like pure gold. Daniel leaned in for a closer look. The light was poor, so he wasn't sure if he was looking at a sequined glove or something else. On closer inspection, he realized the man's appendage really *was* shaped out of gold. An urge to touch it overtook Daniel, and for a moment he forgot about the woman. He leaned across her battered body, desperate to get a closer look at that hand, when she called out:

"Stay away from it!" she wailed at Daniel. "My husband earned that in Viet Nam!"

Daniel blinked at her. "What?"

"He saved a witch doctor's life after the Americans ambushed his village. If you touch it, it will curse you." The woman coughed. Runnels of blood oozed from the corners of her mouth.

Daniel stared at her, slack-jawed, his brain slowly turning over what she'd said, trying to decide if she was delusional from the accident or if he'd misunderstood her. Did she say, *witch doctor*? Daniel giggled. He didn't believe in superstitious drivel. He didn't believe in it when he was earning seven figures and living in a fancy high-rise apartment in Manhattan, sporting Dolce and Gabbana suits and sipping Château d'Yquem at two hundred thousand dollars a bottle. And he didn't believe in it now, when he made his residence inside cardboard boxes in steamy alleyways.

"Nonsense," he muttered, reaching across her twisted body and touching the golden hand anyway.

The surface was cold, like it had just come out of a freezer. The hand was not a medical prosthetic; it was literally precious metal carved to look like a partially opened hand stuck to the stump of the man's wrist.

The old man groaned and clutched at his chest. For a moment Daniel felt sorry for him. But when he considered the Porsche he drove, the expensive tux he was wearing, and the lovely lady dying in the passenger seat beside him, Daniel figured that he'd lived enough of a good life. And it was time now to share it with *him*. Daniel wanted his own good fortune back—*all of it*. The power and prestige. The Life.

And a chunk of gold like that hand would go a long way in helping him escape the streets.

Daniel lifted the man's blood-stained sleeve. "Please," the wounded man spluttered, "don't do it."

Daniel licked his lips and looked around one more time. From far off in the distance he could hear the first faint echo of sirens.

"I'm sorry, pal. They're gonna be here soon. You know how it is." He grabbed hold of the hand and gave it a jerk. It remained stubbornly stuck to his wrist.

"Wait!" The man desperately grabbed Daniel's arm and held it in a vice-like squeeze. "You don't understand."

Daniel could smell the sour mash wafting off his breath. "Understand what, old-timer?"

A sudden light filled the old man's eyes. "My name is Robert Harrington. I was eighteen when they drafted me. I was assigned to Delta Company as a medic, and between the big battles, we'd run an ops called Running the Road. We'd barrel up and down Highway 1 in Vietnam during the dead of night in our M48A3 Patton tanks. We were meant to keep the Viet Cong from planting landmines along the road."

"Did it work?" Daniel couldn't believe he was interested in the man's story, but the old codger still had him in a death grip, so what choice did he have?

"One night we took heavy fire," Harrington continued, oblivious to Daniel's question. "Before I knew it, mortar shells were exploding all around us, and my friends were all killed. I was knocked out cold.

"When I came to, I was being dragged through the jungle. It was the darkest night I'd ever seen it, with no moon to see by, and the VC beat me with their rifles just for the fun of it.

"At last we arrived at what looked like a small makeshift camp. Wounded soldiers lay groaning next to piles of dead bodies. Were it not for a few small cooking fires, I might not have seen their faces. I wish I hadn't. The horror in their eyes…I will never forget it. They haunt me to this day."

The man coughed up a spray of blood, which narrowly missed Daniel's face. The fingers grasping his arm weakened a little. Daniel thought he could've pulled away, but something compelled him to hear the end of the story.

"I was taken to a hut where they brought me to an old man lying on a cot. At first I thought he was a soldier, maybe one of their generals; but when I got a closer look, I realized I'd been mistaken. This was no soldier. His hair was long and white. Long beaded necklaces adorned his leathery neck, with strange pendants hanging off them. He was dressed in robes, and the reverent way the others treated him made me think he was a shaman of sort. He was wounded, his body covered in bloody lacerations. But worst of all was his hand; it was in ruins, torn apart by shrapnel. Although I couldn't understand their gibberish language, I knew what was expected of me. And what would happen if I refused."

"You saved him."

The old man nodded. "I patched up his cuts, set a few broken bones…but the hand was beyond saving." Here he stopped telling his tale and glanced at his golden hand.

"You don't mean…?"

"Yes. They took my hand. It was retribution, you know? He loses his, I lose mine. I get it now. They sliced it off with a machete. Worst pain of my life."

"Then how did you—?"

"I passed out. When I awoke the next day, the VC had abandoned the camp. I was lying on a bunk in the tent where the old man had been. I thought I must have been dreaming, because when I looked down I saw the golden hand, shimmering in the morning light. I didn't feel any pain. I didn't feel much of anything but gratitude to still be alive.

"There was a note on the cot next to me. I couldn't read it then, but I had it translated later. It thanked me for my kind services and for my 'offering.' And it hoped I would accept as payment my new appendage."

Daniel laughed. The story was horrifying, beyond bizarre—yet the man clearly believed it.

The light in Robert Harrington's eyes began to fade. His hand grew so weak that it fell from Daniel's arm, releasing him. Daniel eyed the golden hand greedily. He didn't give a damn about where it came from or how this old geezer got it. He wanted it. It was his ticket out of this life and a chance to get back on his own two feet.

He reached for it…

"The note said one more thing," the man wheezed suddenly.

Daniel hesitated. "What was that?"

"'He who possesses that which does not belong to them shall be cursed.'" The old man eyed Daniel darkly. "The golden hand was meant for me and me alone, and I shall take it to the grave with me."

"Nonsense," Daniel repeated. He reached for the golden hand, noticing it felt even colder now than it had at first. He gave it a hard tug, but it held fast. In case the hand screwed on somehow, Daniel gave it a firm one-quarter turn to the left. To his delight, it snapped off with an audible click.

Daniel brought the hand slowly out of the car and examined it in the lamplight, the dying passengers all but forgotten inside. The sirens were getting closer now. In moments, they'd be at the scene.

As he turned to flee, he heard the woman shout, "Bastard!"

Her husband gave another shudder and pointed his stump at him. "Don't do it," he begged. "It isn't worth what's coming to you!" Then his eyelids fluttered, and his head lolled to one side.

Dead.

The lady noticed her husband's body go limp and started to howl in rage and sorrow. Panicking, Daniel covered her mouth with his hand, trying to shush her, and reassured her that help was on the way. The woman was beyond listening anymore, beyond anything but fighting for survival, and she bit down on Daniel's palm. Enraged, Daniel brought the golden hand down hard across the side of her face. The woman's body slumped forward and lay still. He wiped the blood off his prize and stuffed the hand into his coat pocket.

For good measure, he snatched the woman's purse and the man's wallet and fled the scene before the cops could arrive.

Daniel sat cross-legged in the filth of his Whirlpool condo as the sun rose and the city awoke. He studied the contours of the astonishing golden hand, the fingers and ridges, the delicate design of the hand's joints and fingertips.

Daniel shivered as he remembered the dying man's words. How could some jungle shaman have created such a thing? It had to be worth a small fortune.

He was intrigued about the hand's origins too, not to mention how he could sell it.

But not today. Today he had to lie low.

Safely hidden inside his cardboard condo, Daniel listened to the sirens coming and going. He peered out every now and then to catch a glimpse of the crowd jostling for a view of the bodies. People never change, he thought with a smirk. He heard their aghast voices chattering about the grisly details of the scene.

His scene, he supposed. After all, there might have been one at least one very much alive person to rescue from the smashed car if fate hadn't intervened.

Fate in the name of Daniel P. Simmons, investment banker.

Lover of gold.

He waited till the ruckus died down, which wasn't until almost noon. Then he found a bite to eat in a trash can behind a pizza joint and returned to his box. Fortunately, he didn't see anyone he knew. None of the neighborhood tough guys and gangbangers were out today, probably spooked by the presence of so many cops in their neighborhood. Daniel hated the thugs. They liked to harass the urban campers and steal what little they had. If they found the golden hand…

They would kill him, no doubt.

He shambled back down the filthy alleyway and dove inside his box, closing the flap behind him. Beneath the security of his tattered newspapers he withdrew the golden hand from his pocket and stared longingly at it. *So much gold, so much money.* It was Sunday and the pawn shop at the corner would be closed. He couldn't wait to take it in tomorrow and get it appraised, but would he ever get fair market value for it? Not a chance. What should he do with it then?

What *could* he do?

Daniel was less a believer in fate than he was in opportunity. If he didn't get a fair price for this gold, well, he'd figure something else out in the morning.

He closed his eyes and tried going to sleep. The background noise of the city usually lulled him to sleep.

Sure enough, within seconds he was drifting off, the golden hand clutched to his chest. The hand that grew colder with each passing second.

The sun shines hot and bright in the clear blue sky. He is walking down fifth avenue, but he is all alone. The city stands like an abandoned fortress, lost to time. From behind him he hears a voice calling his name, over and over, a voice that rises and falls like the wind.

Daaaannniiiiel, it whispers.

He looks around but he can't find who's speaking to him. Afraid, he tries to enter a restaurant and then a store to get off the street, but all the doors are locked. The voice grows persistent.

Give me my haaaannnd...

It's like something out of a horror movie, he thinks. The voice is all around him, echoing off the buildings and the empty streets. It's in his head, and his heart is pounding...

Daniel awoke with a jolt.

The golden hand was still pressed against his chest, but even through the layers of grimy clothing he wore, it burned him. It seared his skin like dry ice, and he dropped it, pushing it away. He stared wildly at the thing as he soothed the area where his skin ached.

The memory of the dream still lingered. He could still hear the voice with the unfamiliar accent calling his name and demanding the hand back. But it was *his* hand now, and no one was taking it from him.

"Daaaannniiiiel...."

His heart thudded with terror. The voice sounded real now, stalking the alley outside his box. How could it be so? He wasn't dreaming anymore.

"Give me my haaaannnd..."

Daniel peeked outside.

Nothing. The alley was empty. But he must have been asleep a long time because it was full dark and the traffic has slowed to a trickle. No pedestrians were out either, which wasn't surprising given the fact that this was the crime-infested part of town.

Daniel got up and walked the alley, end to end, looking behind and inside garbage cans, checking the steaming grates, but found no one hiding anywhere. He was completely alone, which should have been reassuring, but somehow it wasn't. Somehow it frightened him worse than ever.

A rustle in the darkness behind him. Daniel pivoted to try to catch a glimpse of what made the noise, but it was gone. It sounded like footsteps, but it was probably the wind.

Yeah, the wind. Logical.

Daniel turned back to his box when another noise stopped him in his tracks.

This time he saw it. Looming at the end of the alley, silhouetted by the orange sodium vapor lamps. A tall shape, like a man's, with grotesquely elongated limbs like a spider's. It took a moment for Daniel's brain to process the image, to make sense of the odd deformity, and it wasn't until the man moved toward him out of the shadows that he realized he had mistaken shadows for arms and legs. The figure was not spider-like, but nor was it a man, either. Not exactly. Where eyes should have been were gouged-out hollows of inky darkness. The mouth was an open pit of toothless blackness. What should have been skin was a sheath of murky translucence, through which Daniel could see outlines of the street beyond.

"*Where's my haaaand?*" it moaned.

Daniel's horror peaked when he saw the machete glinting in the phantom's right hand.

"You can't have it!" Daniel screamed. "It's mine!"

The ghostly figure stopped moving toward him and stared at him. The machete hung in the air. At this closer distance, Daniel could make out long silky strands of white hair on the shape's head.

The witch-doctor.

"*Give me my haaaannnnd,*" it repeated, taking a step closer.

Daniel sunk to his knees, sobbing.

"You can't have it," he said between sobs. "I need it, it's my ticket out of this life! That man, Harrington, he wasn't going to use it anymore, don't you understand? He was all smashed up—he was *dying*—so who cares?"

Daniel closed his eyes as the thing drifted closer.

"Please," he begged.

"Keep it," snarled the voice above him.

Daniel, afraid he misunderstood, opened one eye and looked up at the glowering shaman's spirit.

"W-what?" he said, wiping his eyes.

"I've come for something else."

The machete quivered in the air above him.

"What do you want then?" Daniel asked, trembling.

"Your hand," it hissed at him.

"But you said I could keep it!"

"The *other* hand." The thing revealed the raw stump at the end of its left arm to Daniel.

"There is always a deal to be made, isn't there, Mr. Simmons?"

The machete swung and Daniel screamed.

THE TRAPDOOR

WITH OLIVIA ANN SMITH

Everyone said not to go there. Everyone said not to look there. But one night...I looked.

My name's Jack Cooper, and my family and I just moved into a creepy old house on a hill. We had a long drive from Arizona to New York. I was hungry but our kitchen cupboards were still bare and the refrigerator empty. And my sister Kiley? Still annoying as ever.

"Hey, give those back, JC!" Kiley complained when I grabbed a bag of Doritos out of her hand. She was eating in front of me; what was I supposed to do?

"Ever hear of sharing?" I snapped.

"JC, I need you to help with some boxes!" my mom called from the front door.

Stomping off, I found my mom struggling with some heavy boxes she was hauling in from the truck.

My dad was standing behind her, arguing with the moving guys over something.

"Leave your sister alone," Mom said, frowning at me. "Get these boxes upstairs. And while you're there, you can pick the bedroom you want."

Excited, I grabbed a couple boxes that had my name on them and ran upstairs to have a look before Kiley could pick her room. She'd probably take the biggest one with the most windows and leave me in a stuffy little room with barely enough room for a bed.

There were several rooms to choose from, but most were locked for some reason. One room was quite large and had an old fireplace in it that reminded me of colonial houses before central heating. I figured my parents would want that one. Another was painted an odd shade of pink, and in several spots the paint was peeling, and mold was growing in the corners. I passed on this room. The last room wasn't much better, though. It had a large closet, slanted ceiling, and a big dormer window that looked out over the backyard. I chose this room, even though it was drafty and had a funky smell like wet socks.

All in all, I had to admit I was unimpressed with this house. On the outside, the mansion had the appearance of a miniature castle, with dark stone walls, turrets, and sprawling gardens. It looked pretty cool on the realtor's website, and when I showed my friends back home, I could sense their jealousy, like I was some kind of big shot moving up in the world.

But on the inside it was dark, dingy, and uninviting. I felt watched everywhere I went, even when Kiley and my parents were nowhere around. I felt small and lonely and a million miles away from anything that made sense.

Would I ever get used to this place? A part of me was afraid the answer was no.

My parents and I argued a lot, which I guess is typical of most teenagers.

Tonight we were arguing about moving to New York. I told them over dinner I didn't want to be here, but my mom shot back that I was being unfair and disrespectful. My dad was starting a new job at a big company in Rochester. He would be gone most days and plenty of nights, and he needed Kiley and me to be supportive during this tough time of settling in. Besides, he said with his usual lopsided grin, I'd get to experience my first winter—with real snow!—in just a few months.

Great.

I took my sour mood upstairs and went to bed. My bed wasn't made yet, but I didn't care. I flopped down onto the mattress and closed my eyes.

This day couldn't be over fast enough.

I must have fallen asleep, because when I opened my eyes again the sun was gone, and my room was blacker than the bottom of a well.

I heard a rattling sound. It sounded like it was coming up through the walls. From the basement maybe? I climbed out of bed and put my ear to the radiator, listening.

All of a sudden I heard a scream! It sounded like a girl in pain, but I knew instinctively it wasn't Kiley. Terrified, I jumped back into bed and curled up into a ball. No way was I going down there alone to investigate.

I didn't know who was screaming in the house, but the secret would soon be discovered.

~~~

That week, I started at my new public school. Compared to the little private school I attended in Arizona, this place was enormous. I felt like a little fish swimming through endless currents of students, most of whom scowled at the stranger in their midst.

For three days nobody talked to me. How was I ever going to learn where everything was? Or who I could trust?

As I sat in math class one day, I looked around at the new faces and wondered what my friends back home were doing. I missed the routine of my old life. In Arizona, there were no screaming girls in the basement. Who was she? Why was she in my basement? I wished I could talk to someone. By someone I meant *anyone* besides Kiley or my parents. Someone who might actually believe me and not laugh in my face.

"Hey, you're the new kid, right?" A boy sat down next to me. He had greasy brown hair, green eyes, and wore a black leather jacket. I noticed his math book looked spotless, like it hadn't been opened all year.

"Yeah, I'm Jack, but my friends call me JC. Who are you?"

"I'm Jacob. You moved into the house on the hill, right?"

"That's right."

"The old Robertson place." He grinned like he knew a secret. "At least that's what they call it, among other things."

Among other things. I made a mental note to follow up on that comment later.

"I haven't been sleeping too well the past few nights," I said, yawning.

"Not surprised," he said. "If I lived there, I wouldn't be able to sleep at all."

"Why?"

"Tell you later."

After class, I followed Jacob to the lunchroom and sat down at a table where we could finish our conversation in private.

"So my house has a reputation," I said, nibbling a piece of pizza.

"It has a lot more than a reputation," Jacob replied. He leaned in and whispered, "It's practically a legend around here."

"What makes you say that?"

"The story goes that a long time ago a girl was playing dolls in the basement. She discovered a trapdoor and opened it, but she lost her balance and fell. Today, when people live there, they can still hear her screams as she fell into the pit. She must have died, but no one knows for sure. They never found a body."

I asked, "What was the girl's name?"

"Annabelle Robertson." Jacob glanced around as if afraid someone might overhear. I found his anxiety curious. What could he possibly be afraid of?

"I know what you're thinking," he said, finishing off his milk and crushing the carton. "I'm not afraid or nothin', I just don't like saying her name out loud. You know?"

I raised my eyebrows skeptically.

"It's the curse, that's all."

"Curse?" I felt a cold chill drip down the back of my neck.

"Yeah," he said. "No one ever seems to last long in your house. They move in, they move out like a month or two later. Everyone knows about it. Your house is haunted, dude."

"There are no such things as ghosts."

Jacob shook his head. "Not ghosts—a *witch*. Long time ago there was a colonial settlement here. For a while, the people almost didn't survive. Droughts, blight, and long cold winters killed over half the settlers in the village. Your house stands on a spot where an old woman used to live alone, and they accused her of witchcraft. They suspected her of casting spells over the village and burying the bodies of her enemies under her cabin. They burned her house down and ran her out of the settlement. But she swore she'd be back for her vengeance, and it would cost the lives of three local children. Their blood would make her young and powerful. And immortal."

I must have been staring at Jacob with uncomfortable intensity because he laughed and said, "Of course, it's just a stupid story. Probably not true at all."

Probably. I chewed my pizza thoughtfully. Curses, witches, and haunted houses. How was it possible? Sure, the other night was strange. I thought I heard a screaming girl, but it was also my first night in a new house. How did I know what the pipes sounded like? Or the way the timbers of the old house settled?

Weren't those the natural explanations for weird sounds in an old house?

"All right," I said, deciding to play along. I liked Jacob. Making a real friend in the first week of school would be quite an accomplishment. "What did this girl Annabelle supposedly look like?"

"She had red hair, sparkling blue eyes, and loved the color yellow!"

"How do you know so much about her?"

"Because Annie was my cousin—or *was*!"

I stared at Jacob, trying to figure out if he was joking or not. He looked sincere, even grief-stricken, so I decided to invite him to spend the night. Maybe it would bring him a little comfort?

"You mean tonight?" he asked, suddenly interested.

"Sure. It's Friday, I doubt my folks will mind. They'll be thrilled that I'm not being some sort of hermit and I actually talked to someone."

"You got a deal, JC."

When Jacob arrived that night, I greeted him at the door. He was lugging a large, heavy-looking backpack over his shoulder.

"What's with the backpack?" I asked.

"It's my equipment," he said eagerly.

"Equipment for what?"

"You know, infrared camera, digital recorder, full-spectrum analysis stuff. Ghost hunting equipment!"

I looked around to make sure my parents or Kiley were out of earshot. Talk of "ghost hunting" would've worried them and led to all sorts of unwanted questions. Kiley would probably have nightmares for a week and blame it all on me. She was only ten and easily spooked.

"Where did you get all this stuff?" I asked as I led him upstairs to my room.

"My dad's been doing paranormal investigating as a hobby ever since my cousin died. He's wanted to investigate this place forever, but the previous owners wouldn't let him. You have no idea how badly he wanted to come here tonight!"

Jacob slung his backpack onto my bed and unzipped it. He took out a funny-looking device. "What is that?" I asked.

"It's a digital recorder," he explained. "You use it to catch EVPs, or ghost voices."

"And what's that?"

"This?" He held up a black box with a white screen and red needle on the top. "It's an EMF detector. It measures the electromagnetic field in a room. Ghosts are said to generate their own electricity; that's why people feel chills, cold spots, or goosebumps when a ghost is around." He pulled out the rest of his equipment: video cameras, thermal cameras, and more handheld devices like the EMF detector.

I wandered over to the radiator under the window and pointed down to the floor. "This is where I heard her. I was asleep when her screams woke me up."

Jacob got a faraway look in his eyes. "My cousin," he said quietly.

55

"You don't think…" I started to say.

"What?"

"Nothing." Suddenly my mom's voice called from the staircase. It was dinner time and she wanted us to come down.

"I'll talk to you about it later," I promised.

After dinner, Jacob and I chilled in my bedroom for the rest of the evening and played Xbox. We waited for my parents and Kiley to go to bed.

Around midnight we switched everything off and listened to the quiet of the house. Jacob knelt down by the radiator in the same spot where I had heard the scream and listened intently. Except for the moaning wind outside, the house was silent.

I hoped my friend wasn't going to think this was all just a big waste of time.

"What were you going to say earlier before dinner?" he asked, still looking at the floor.

"Nothing, really. I was just thinking, is there any chance Annabelle could still be…?" I couldn't bring myself to finish the sentence.

Jacob looked surprised. "Alive?"

I shrugged, my cheeks burning. "I know, it's stupid."

"It's been over ten years, dude. How would it be possible?" But even as he said it, a look of hope dawned on his face.

He walked over to the bed and started rummaging through his gear. He handed me a digital recorder, flashlight and a camera, and kept the EMF detector, a thermal camera, and another flashlight for himself. Armed with state-of-the-art ghost hunting equipment, we crept out of my bedroom and down the stairs to the basement.

"Do you smell that?" Jacob asked as we opened the door to the basement and started descending the steps. His nose wrinkled in disgust. "I think it's mold."

"No, it's something else." I didn't know what exactly, but I didn't want to speculate. It smelled much worse than mold.

My parents hadn't replaced the lightbulbs down here yet, so we had to rely on our flashlights. We switched them on. Twin beams of yellow light carved open the darkness, revealing a basement in dire need of attention.

"Look at that!" Jacob pointed.

I gasped. Green slimy water oozed down the basement walls. Jacob yanked his shirt up over his mouth and nose. Not a bad idea. Who knew how much black mold and deadly spores were growing on the walls down here?

We pushed on deeper into the basement, scanning every inch of the place with our flashlights. There was lots of old junk left from previous owners. Chests of old clothes pushed off to the sides. More than once we stepped in smelly puddles of water that leached up from the floor and got our sneakers wet.

"They should condemn this place," I heard Jacob say when we reached the other side of the basement.

I couldn't agree more.

Jacob turned on his EMF detector and it immediately started to crackle and squeal.

"I've got a hit!" he exclaimed excitedly.

"Does that mean there's a ghost here?" I asked. I started taking pictures with the night vision camera he gave me.

"Possibly. Let's keep looking," he said.

We explored the rest of the basement. We inspected every corner and even looked under the cobweb-strewn stairs. Then something caught Jacob's eye.

"Hey, did we look behind those boxes yet?" he asked, pointing to a pile of dingy boxes over near the furnace.

"Not yet," I said.

We carefully stepped up to the boxes, shifting them to the side so we could look behind and under them, when Jacob suddenly cried out, "Eww! Look at that big pile of green slime!"

I stared. Was that a girl's handprint in the middle of it?

"Maybe the trapdoor is under the slime," I said.

"I'm not touching that nasty stuff!" said Jacob.

I had an idea. I ripped open one of the old boxes and used its lid as a shovel to scoop the green slime away. Beneath the layers of muck, we saw the outline of what looked like a door latch.

"I think you found the trapdoor!" Jacob leaned toward it for a closer look. "It definitely looks old."

"What should we do?"

Jacob looked up at me like I was crazy. "What do you think? We should open it, that's what!"

We found a couple of old rags and used them to grip the trapdoor latch so we wouldn't have to touch the slime.

At first, the door wouldn't budge. Probably rusted shut. Together, we gave another big heave and suddenly the door sprang open! A gasp of dank air blew out at us.

Jacob shined his flashlight down the shaft, but the beam was immediately swallowed up by the thick darkness. "Whoa! It's gotta be forty or fifty feet deep down there; maybe more."

"There are no steps on the side to climb down it," I observed.

"Then we need rope."

"My dad has some out in the shed. Wait here."

Jacob shook his head furiously. "No way, dude, I'm coming with you!"

We made our way back upstairs. The rest of the house was still at peace. I thought I could even hear my sister's buzz saw snoring floating down from her bedroom.

We got the rope from the shed and quickly returned to the basement. Tension knotted my stomach. Were we doing the right thing? What was at the bottom of the shaft? I had visions of rats the size of small dogs scuffling around down there, pink eyes glaring in the dark and sharp little teeth clicking hungrily.

I was about to say something to Jacob when he blurted, "Tie the rope to that beam over there."

I did as he said, not wanting to look weak in front of my new friend, but I had my doubts. Serious doubts. This was way more dangerous than it seemed. If the rope broke, or if we got stuck somehow down in that hole...we could die.

I pushed those nagging worries aside and handed the rope to Jacob. I tied the other end securely to the support beam.

"Here goes nothin'," he said, and dropped the rope into the hole.

We waited, holding our breaths, for the rope to splat on the floor below. But instead the rope, like the flashlight, vanished into that total blackness under our house. I swallowed hard and looked at Jacob.

For the first time, I saw fear in his eyes.

"What do you want to do?" I asked him.

He looked away. "I don't know. It's your house. What do *you* want to do?"

"How deep do you think it is?"

"Your rope was at least fifty feet long, and it never reached the bottom. It could go on forever."

I doubted that but I didn't say anything.

We made up our minds. Jacob started down the shaft first. The plan was when he reached the bottom, he would explore a little bit, take pictures with his night vision and infrared cameras, and then climb back up with my help. I watched nervously as his feet slipped a couple times on the damp walls of the shaft. It looked like it was dug out of bedrock, and judging by the saturation, there must have been water down at the bottom someplace.

I considered for a moment that this might be a well, but who dug a well in the basement of a house? And besides, this house wasn't old enough to have a well.

Pacing the floor nervously, I waited for some sign that Jacob had made it to the bottom of the hole. I kept looking over my shoulder at the stairs, expecting at any moment to see my mother or father standing there, aghast. I'd probably be grounded until my senior year.

As I was envisioning spending the rest of my high school career in my bedroom, the rope gave a jerk, and I heard my friend's voice call from below. "I've made it! I'm in some kind of a chamber. I think it's—"

His voice cut off. My heart lurched and started beating wildly.

"Jacob? Jacob, can you hear me? What's going on down there?"

Then excitedly, "You have to come down here, JC! You have to see this for yourself!"

―❦―

Biting down hard to keep my teeth from chattering, I lowered myself slowly into the shaft. I couldn't help but wonder if this was what cave explorers felt the first time they descended into the earth. Did they fear they'd never see the light of day again? That the earth would suddenly reject their presence and crush them under tons of rock? I knew that wouldn't happen, that I was letting my emotions get away from me, but I couldn't shake my sense of dread.

Something was wrong and we shouldn't be here. This feeling clawed at my gut with relentless force.

When my feet finally reached the bottom, I exhaled a sigh of gratitude. Up above me I could only see darkness, but behind me…

Jacob stood in an aura of light cast by a circle of candles on the floor. Strange symbols were carved on the floor in the middle of the candles: geometric shapes, lines and arrows, and a few that looked like animals or maybe some type of ancient writing. I went over to Jacob and put my hand on his shoulder. His eyes looked absorbed by the appearance of the strange ritual site, as though he were in some kind of trance.

"Jacob, what is this pl—?" I started to say when a girl's scream interrupted me! It echoed through the stone chamber we stood in, piercing my eardrums. We shined our flashlights all around, but we were alone in the chamber.

"That was the same screaming I heard last night in my bedroom!" I told him. "Now it sounds like it's coming through the walls."

Jacob dug the EMF detector out of his pocket and flipped it on. It beeped and chirped a little, but it wasn't recording any unusual electromagnetic activity. I started taking still shots with the night vision camera I carried around my neck.

"I'm not getting anything," Jacob reported as he turned on his thermal camera. "The temperature down here is 62 degrees, but it isn't rising or falling."

"What do you think it means?" I asked him, afraid of what the answer could be.

Jacob looked thoughtful. "Maybe there are no ghosts down here after all."

"You mean..."

"Annabelle could still be alive."

A spike of fear drove through my chest.

"We should look for a secret passage of some kind," he suggested.

I nodded. Although my feet felt like two heavy bricks, I helped Jacob feel along the stone walls for any sort of lever or other clue that might reveal a hidden passageway. As we searched carefully, a glint of something shiny caught my eye on the far wall. I went over to inspect it and found a framed photograph of a girl crying while being chained to a wall.

"Hey, look at this." I showed Jacob the picture. He immediately took it down off the wall. Behind it was an oddly shaped rock that looked like it didn't belong in the wall. Jacob applied pressure on the rock and a huge stone wall opened up. Jacob and I stepped through into a room where three sets of brass chains hung off the walls. In one set of shackles stood a girl about eighteen years old, with red hair and blue eyes! Her face was pale, her eyes dark and gloomy. Her long, bedraggled hair fell in twisted clumps around her shoulders. Jacob and I approached the girl warily.

"What happened and why are you here?" I asked.

The girl shouted, "Go away!" in a hoarse voice.

"What is your name?" Jacob said.

The girl's face projected the deepest sorrow I had ever seen. "Anna. My name is Anna, and you better leave while you still can."

"Anna… Annabelle? Are you my cousin?" Jacob's eyes widened in surprise.

I glanced over my shoulder, suddenly afraid of specters emerging from the gloom. "What do you mean, 'while you still can'? Is there somebody else down here with us?"

A bang echoed behind us.

"What was that?" Jacob drew closer to me as we shone our flashlights all around this nightmarish torture chamber.

"She's coming! She's coming!" Annabelle cackled madly, her chains clanking against the stone wall. She sounded like an inmate at an asylum. "You better run! Momma won't like you down here with me!" She tipped her head back and laughed again, the sound like knife blades stabbing my brain.

"Anna, no, you have to come with us…" Jacob started to say; but his cousin, if indeed she was still his cousin, kept up her howling until the din drowned out his voice. He tried to rip the chains off the wall and free her, but they were stuck on tight.

"Leave me alone!" Annabelle Robertson, the girl who fell down the hole in the basement floor ten years ago, stared murderously at Jacob and me.

"Something's wrong with her," I told Jacob, but my friend was shaking his head in denial. "I think she's insane. We have to get out of here…*now*!"

"I can't leave her," he insisted.

"She's coming, and now it's too late," sputtered Annabelle.

"Who's coming?" I looked all around frantically.

"Momma! Momma is coming! *Look, there she is!*"

From a slight opening in the wall that we didn't notice before, the bent and twisted figure of a hideous woman appeared in the chamber. She had sunken black eyes and cracked lips the color of blood. Soiled rags fit loosely over a bony frame that popped with each movement of her disjointed limbs. Her body contorted and twisted in sickening ways as she scuttled closer to us. It wasn't merely extreme age that warped her body; she had adopted the form of a human-spider hybrid to survive in the dark all these years.

Your house stands on a spot where an old woman used to live alone, and they accused her of witchcraft. They suspected her of casting spells over the village and burying the bodies of her enemies under her cabin. They burned her house down and ran her out of the settlement. But she swore she'd be back for her vengeance, and it would cost the lives of three local children. Their blood would make her young and powerful. And immortal.

Immortality.

This old witch was immortal and lived under my house.

Now we knew who the other two shackles were for.

THE INCIDENT

"Rose, your mother is missing."

It all starts with these five words in a cell phone call. Simple words, really. Each one weightless and trivial—but together, a hammer blow to the soul.

In an instant, my world fragments, and I am falling, falling into blackness.

I faint, and when I wake up, on a dirty sidewalk outside a café surrounded by camera-flashing strangers, I am told everything will be all right.

They lie, of course.

Nothing will ever be the same again.

Miranda, my former governess and now one of my closest friends, comforts me nightly by sitting at my bedside. I enjoy her company and companionship.

She was born in Haiti in the small coastal town of Petit Goave and later adopted by a British ambassador. She has an odd yet charming accent, a mix of Haitian Creole and British sophistication, as my mother likes to say. Her skin is dark and smooth, her eyes a stunning jade. Along with teaching me the conjugation of verbs and the subtleties of society, she has opened up a world the likes of which I had no idea existed beyond the stately walls of this mansion.

My mother has always been terribly busy with her job. Likewise, my father is a ghost who shows up in my life now and again, but drifts away before I can get too close to him. Yet Miranda has always been there for me.

The one constant in my life.

"Would you like more tea, Rose?" Miranda asks, noticing my empty cup. Thirteen years of loyal service and friendship. She probably knows more of my family's secrets than I do.

"No, thank you, Miranda." I smile sweetly at her.

"Then I shall leave you to rest."

"No," I say quickly. "Please stay."

At my request, she helps me stand from bed. A deep and profound exhaustion pervades my body. My normally secluded life is turned upside down. Constant interviews with journalists, two live TV appearances on CNN and NBC News, and ceaseless phone calls have taken their toll on me. Yet I must get to the bottom of what happened to my mother. Wouldn't she do the same for me, spare no resource in finding me and bringing me home?

We cross the room to two comfortable rocking chairs angled in front of the fireplace. The night has a chill to it, so she starts a fire in the hearth and settles into the chair beside me.

"Are you feeling all right, Rose?" she asks tenderly, rubbing my arm.

I meet her gaze. "There is something you haven't told me about that night in Haiti." The trip to Haiti was a birthday gift for Miranda. Originally, I was supposed to travel with them to her homeland, but preparations for Stanford in the fall kept me at home. My mother accompanied her instead. It was a sweet gesture but with ulterior motives.

Miranda frowns. "I'm not sure I know what you mean."

"You told me about a crowd and that you turned your back for only a minute, and when you looked again..."

"She was gone," she finishes.

"How could that have happened?"

Miranda looks uncomfortable with the question. "Haiti is not always a safe place. There are gangs who murder and kidnap foreigners."

"There are gangs who do that everywhere," I object. "Surely, if someone took my mother, you would have heard a scream...*something*."

"I don't know what you want me to say."

"It just doesn't add up."

Two weeks ago I flew to Haiti to hear for myself the details of the investigation from the Police Nationale d'Haiti. I met the detective assigned to the case, Ricardo Estime, who filled me in on the scant details. He wore annoyance about him like other men wear cologne, and he lost patience quickly for my endless questions.

Eventually, I accepted his promise to call if anything turned up, and I returned home, thoroughly disappointed by his apparent indifference to the case and lack of any leads. It was as though my mother vanished into thin air.

"I think you should be careful," Miranda says, catching my eye. "Your questions might arouse suspicion."

"What would be suspicious about a daughter looking for her mother?"

Miranda turns away from me and stares at the crackling fire. "It terrifies me to talk about it, much less recall everything that happened. I've never seen anything like it in my life. I suggest you let it go."

"I am not a child anymore, Miranda." I hope my tone conveys the urgency of the matter.

"I understand that."

"Then tell me what you know."

Miranda sighs deeply. I wait for her to speak.

"You've seen your mother's study," she says.

I nod slowly, unsure where she is going. "Yes. I was not permitted to go in there, but that didn't stop me."

It wasn't easy betraying my mother's trust. I was twelve—old enough to know better, young enough to do it anyway. I stole the spare key from the jewelry box in her bedroom and snuck into her private space. I was shocked. The walls were covered floor to ceiling with newspaper cutouts, posters, maps, and photographs showing strange objects in the sky. Some were daytime shots, where the objects looked dark and heavily pixelated. Others were taken at night, and showed craft of different shapes and sizes, with lights of varying colors and intensities. Some lights flew in clusters; others were solitary, hovering in the sky like beacons to humanity.

Or warnings.

I knew at once what I was looking at, but I couldn't put into words what I was thinking. My mother was investigating UFOs. And she'd been apparently doing it for years.

From that moment on I kept a close eye on her. When she wasn't plying her trade as the executive director of the biggest financial consulting firm in Connecticut, she was tracking flying saucer data, mapping the locations, and collaborating with other ufologists from around the world. Sometimes distraught strangers showed up on our doorstep, and she'd spirit them away to the parlor or the library for a lengthy tête-à-tête.

When this happened, I would stand outside the door and listen, amazed at what I heard. Alien abductions. Experimentation. Time lapses. Unknown wounds on the body.

Disappearances.

Then came the Haitian sightings. Witnesses in the suburb of Petionville witnessed strange craft roaming the sky for several nights in a row, similar to the triangle-shaped Phoenix Lights that soared in complete silence over Arizona and Nevada in 1997. Needless to say, my mother's interest was piqued.

The trip to Haiti was supposed to be a birthday present for Miranda, but in reality it was a ruse to get down there and check things out for herself.

"What does my mother's office have to do with anything?"

"I think she stumbled onto something she shouldn't have. If I tell you what I know, you need to promise me something."

"Anything."

Miranda swallows hard and says, "Promise me we'll destroy it."

I feel a vague fear clutch at my chest. "You mean her office?"

"All of it."

"I promise you. We'll get rid of everything. We'll do it together."

"Tonight?"

I hesitate, then nod. If getting rid of all my mother's papers means that much to Miranda, then it is the least I could do. "Of course."

Satisfied, Miranda settles back into her chair to tell her tale.

She tells it slowly, stopping often to choose her words carefully, though I have no doubt the memory has long legs and wanders nightly through her dreams.

"Our plane landed in Toussaint Louverture International Airport in Port-au-Prince just after sunrise," she begins, "but the day was already unbearably hot…"

This is Miranda's story.

Upon landing in Port-au-Prince and checking into their hotel, Miranda immediately contacted a childhood friend of hers, a man by the name of Jean-Eders Laveau. He was a merchant who lived in the wealthy suburb of Petionville, in the clean breezy hills overlooking the sprawling streets of Port-au-Prince.

They traveled to see him in a crowded tap tap, the tropical heat already as heavy as a moist blanket hanging about their necks.

The smells of the teeming city, occasionally pungent with garbage and manure depending on the location, changed to sweet open air when they reached Petionville. There they found the high-spirited Jean-Eders, waving to them from the portico of his impressive villa. He had an adventure planned for them that evening—an adventure, he told them, they would not soon forget.

He asked them if they were interested in seeing a private Vodou ceremony, one in which few Westerners, to his knowledge, had ever participated. As a connoisseur of the paranormal, I knew my mother would have found such a diversion pleasurable.

Eager, they accompanied Jean-Eders to the small coastal town of Petit Goave where he owned a shipping business, forty miles south of Port-au-Prince on the Southern Peninsula. He had many close friends there. He was well liked and respected for his humane treatment of the poor, and the fact he brought many jobs to the area.

Jean-Eders was told recently by a trustworthy friend that a Vodou ceremony was planned for that evening to help an ailing boy possessed by a demon *loa*, or spirit of the underworld. What intrigued my mother the most, according to Miranda, was the fact that the boy's symptoms started right after the first sighting of the UFOs. This fact did not escape Jean-Eders, either. In fact, unexplained mutilations of livestock were also reported on the property where the boy lived.

By the time my mother, Miranda, and Jean-Eders arrived at a small rural shack on the outskirts of town, most of the ceremony participants had already assembled, including the houngan priest. A row of young male drummers stood on short ladders behind their massive instruments, pounding out ancient tribal rhythms that echoed like thunder over their heads. A trio of female priestesses called *mambos* danced and shouted with abandon around a roaring fire.

Jean-Eders left them to go talk with the boy's parents, Renauld and Lydie Tunis. When he returned, he relayed to them what he'd learned. The boy, Jacques, had been acting strangely. Fearful of the dark. Wandering at night. Savagely kicking and spitting at anyone who came too close. The other villagers were afraid of him, called him the devil, and said Papa Gede, the god of death, had possessed his body.

My mother thought it sounded more like trauma, the behavior of a child who'd experienced something terrifying and knew no better way of dealing with his inflamed emotions. But to the locals, whose religious practices were woven into the fabric of their lives, all of it could be explained by demonic possession.

The ceremony began a few minutes later with the ritualistic sacrifice of a chicken to Papa Legba, the god who controls the passageway between the physical and spiritual worlds. The boy thrashed and screamed during this part of the ceremony, requiring four stout young men to hold down his arms and legs. His eyes blazed red, and blood seeped from his mouth as if he'd bitten his tongue, a distinct possibility given his outbursts. After the houngan made the sacrifice and poured the blood from the severed chicken's neck into the fire, he crept closer to Jacques, his wide eyes peering through the slits of his painted ceremonial mask. The boy's paroxysms intensified until it seemed his arms would rip off his shoulders.

    The houngan mumbled some odd Haitian Creole words Miranda didn't recognize and sprinkled some clear liquid onto the boy's forehead. Upon contact with his feverish skin, the liquid quickly dissipated into smoke, but not before scalding the boy and leaving scars. Jacques screamed again, bucking his hips and thrusting his shoulders up, almost freeing himself from the terrified men who visibly struggled against the preternatural strength in the skinny ten-year-old's body, before sinking to the ground and falling unconscious.

    At that moment, a series of bright lights appeared on the horizon. The ritual stopped at once as everyone stared with wonder up at the objects moving silently across the night sky. They were each long and conical shaped, and they split off into smaller lights, which darted around the sky like fireflies. They made a sound like a whirring hum, but no obvious source of propulsion could be seen. They danced and flitted and eventually reassembled into a larger craft, which lingered in the air before slowly descending.

The boy awoke with a startled shriek, and this time there was the popping of bone and ripping of tendon as he dislocated both shoulders and squirmed away from his distracted captors. He tried to run, but as soon as he gained his feet, a beam of light shot from the alien craft and struck him in the back. Jacques collapsed to the ground. He curled up into a ball, covering his face from the blinding ray, whimpering, and sobbing for help. No one moved. The light beam acted as a magnet and started pulling the boy toward the alien craft—and still no one intervened to help the boy.

Except my mother. She couldn't let the boy be taken away like this. She leapt in front of him, blocking the beam, but still the ship drew him in closer. She attempted to grab hold of Jacques' waist to pull him back, but an ear-splitting mechanical screech, followed by a searing blast of heat as the light beam intensified, forced her to drop the boy. The beam widened, probing for both of them now, and within a few seconds both my mother and Jacques were drawn inside the craft. The light source cut out and the ship went dark again. It rose slowly, rotated on its axis, and pointed itself to the north. Then, without so much as disturbing a blade of grass, it shot away like a bullet fired through a silencer and was gone.

The fire has died to just a few glowing embers by the time Miranda finishes her tale. The moon is out, and a bar of pale light strikes the floor near my feet. A lone star hangs in the sky below the moon.

A calm repose settles over Miranda as we sit together in the darkness. She looks relieved for the story to be over. I don't blame her. The burden will be hers to carry for a long time, but at least I can do something for her.

"We'll have a fire tomorrow," I remind her, reaching out to hold my friend's hand.

"A bonfire," she agrees, a faint smile growing on her lips.

"We'll burn all her work," I continue, my eagerness rising. "I want it gone, all of it, every last file, every book, every photograph she has ever collected. Not a trace of her mad obsession will be left behind."

Miranda stares strangely at me.

"Why are you looking at me like that?" I ask.

"Do you really think that will change anything?"

I don't know what to say. "Of course. We'll start over. No more UFOs, no more paranormal. Maybe Father will return to normal again."

"Normal." Miranda says it like it's a word she's never heard of before. "I don't think you understand."

Her words begin to slow down, the syllables stretch out and the vowels blend together, like she's speaking underwater.

"I don't want to burn the papers in her office," Miranda says, standing up. Something in her face is changing, too. The color...her skin...has a sheen of gray I've never noticed before. "We mean to burn the house down."

"We?"

The star outside grows bigger and brighter. The orb shines with a brilliant blue intensity. Miranda gets up and moves to the window.

"You need to come with us," she says.

"What is happening?"

"It's time."

"I don't understand."

"They sent me back for you, Rose. Your mother is summoning you." Miranda rushes up to me and grips my arms painfully. Dark liquid floods her eyes and makes them gleam like inkwells.

Just then the window crashes open and a gust of hot air blows into the room. I see the others enter my bedroom behind Miranda, surrounding us: tall, spindly beings with bulbous heads and heavily wrinkled skin like an elephant's. Huge circular insect eyes protrude from their elongated skulls. Their mouths are thin slashes from which a sweet-smelling vapor exudes, making my head feel light and airy. They encircle me, their hands rubbing against my body with cold, oily fingers. One of them touches my face with a greasy palm and covers my mouth as they carry me out to the light. I try to fight, but there are too many of them.

From somewhere far away I smell smoke. The house is burning. By morning it will be a smoldering shell, and I will be far, far away. A story on someone else's bulletin board, a new obsession for a troubled soul to worry over.

An incident with no explanation or clues to follow, except for a strange light in the sky.

THE LIGHTHOUSE

Maine, 1869

The fog sat like a heavy veil on the cold, steely waters of the North Atlantic. Every now and then a strong breeze stirred the mist, which sent hazy phantoms twirling toward our boat, their damp fingers reaching down the back of my thick wool coat and chilling my spine.

Shivering, I blew on my hands and looked at the oarsman, a rugged looking sea dog named Wharton, who propelled our skiff with great earnest and not a little terror as we approached the fog-shrouded coastline of Shaw Island. The island, named after the first keeper who served there fifty years ago, brooded in eerie gray silence. Although its isolation in infamously treacherous waters would give many men pause, I looked forward to my duties as the new lighthouse keeper. I grew up in the small Maine town of Kennebunkport and spent my youth on wharves watching shipbuilders create some of the mightiest vessels in the world. I wanted nothing more than to protect the brave souls who sailed past my island from the shoals and rock ledges that threatened every passing ship.

"You're sweating profusely," I noted of the oarsman.

"'Tis not the effort that dampens my brow, Mr. Abbott," he replied in a gravelly voice.

I followed his gaze and noticed the dark silhouette of the lighthouse slowly emerging from the fog. "I see our destination awaits," I said, glancing back at Wharton. "You don't like the place?"

"I prefer it better from a distance, sir."

I frowned. "Surely an experienced mariner like yourself doesn't believe the tales?"

"I believe what happens at the Crow ain't natural."

'Crow' or 'Crow Island' was the nickname given to the island by superstitious locals. A flock of crows was called a murder, and not because of their tendency to feast on the dead. Instead, according to folklore, crows would gather to decide the fate of an injured or sick member of their flock.

Usually, that decision was death.

I was not surprised that Wharton shared this opinion of the island. Its history of misfortune and untimely deaths was well established in these parts. However, my own experiences and education in the science of naval vessels and the sea forbade such absurdity, but I wouldn't hold it against Wharton, whom I liked very much.

The old sailor's ruddy face turned pale as he guided the skiff up to the island's little wooden mooring.

"You'd do well to remember that this place is cursed," Wharton said after we'd docked. "There've been suicides here. The last keeper even went mad and attacked his own family. Blood was found on the walls and floor of every room, as if he hunted them down like prey. When it was over, he threw himself from the top of the lighthouse. But his wife and children…they weren't so lucky, sir. Their deaths were slow and brutal."

Wharton crossed himself before continuing.

"Not a seaman from here to Newport Harbor ain't heard somethin' afoul about this place. If it weren't for your generous payment and my missus needin' nice things, I wouldn't have brought you."

"Your interest in my well-being is duly noted and appreciated," I remarked as I grabbed my two bags and stepped off the skiff.

"You seem like a good man, Mr. Abbot," Wharton commented. "Your rise from midshipman to second lieutenant on board the *USS Chesapeake* is well known. Like your father, a fine seaman and lighthouse keeper in his own right, you know more about the sea than most men alive. But the Crow ain't like most places, and the sea 'round here has its own way of draggin' men down."

"I hope to see you again soon, my friend," I said, touched by his concern.

"Aye." With one last anxious glance up at the towering lighthouse, Wharton pushed off without another word. I watched him row away quickly until he vanished into the fog.

After Wharton's departure, I turned my attention to the woefully dilapidated lighthouse. After many years of brutal treatment by the sea, its stone edifice had chunks of rock missing and was stained black with mold. The wind and waves had, over the years, shifted many of the large boulders on the small island, giving Shaw Island a reckless, wild appearance.

A small skiff lay beached next to the lighthouse. Upon closer inspection it appeared to be in good working order, for which I was grateful. Tomorrow I would need to row to the mainland for provisions, weather providing. The coast of Maine was half a mile to the west, and I was sure I could pick up everything I needed in Cape Elizabeth.

Satisfied to know I had means of transport, I started up the gravel path to the surprisingly commodious house attached to the back of the lighthouse tower. As I walked, I stole a glance up at the lantern room and noticed a shadow slide across the glass.

I stopped.

The shadow moved again, and I could distinctly make out a head and possibly the torso of a man. Startled, I dropped my bags. The dark form moved swiftly from side to side, as though searching for something—and then, as quickly I discerned it, it vanished!

I took a few deep breaths to calm my racing heart. What a fool I was being, no doubt influenced by Wharton's superstition. The light was surely playing tricks with my eyes. There were a hundred natural explanations for what I'd just seen, and one surely would present itself when I climbed the steps to the lantern room and inspected it for myself.

Wharton's mention of the last keeper and the mysterious circumstances surrounding his fate weighed heavily on my mind. Yes, staying at a place where a grisly murder had occurred disturbed me, as it would most men with a considerate temperament. But that didn't change the fact that for some men, even accompanied by family, lighthouse duties could be a heavy burden. For some, isolation and the ocean's cold indifference to human suffering frayed their nerves and led to mental breakdown.

That was it. A rational explanation for what had happened to the former keeper and his family.

Madness...and murder.

I continued along the path to the back of the house. It, too, needed repair; but what sank my spirits was not the condition of the house but the size of the island.

Shaw Island was a tiny spit of land. There was neither tree nor shrub, and hardly a single blade of grass. The surface was rocky and irregular. My hope for a vegetable garden and a self-sustaining lifestyle were immediately dashed. It appeared I would be making frequent trips across the bay for supplies and provisions.

Sighing, I entered the house. The door opened to a spartan but otherwise comfortable communal area. On the right was a small kitchen area with a stove, cupboards, and a small table. Ahead was a living area consisting of a faded green davenport and a reading chair set on a threadbare rug in front of a stone hearth. To my left a wooden staircase led up to the second-floor bedrooms. Next to it stood a narrow entryway with its own set of steps spiraling up the lighthouse tower to the lantern room.

As soon as I got myself settled in, I would see at once to the lamp, which was no doubt in need of serious repair.

I set my bags down on the kitchen table and inspected the cupboards. As I'd suspected, the cupboards were bare, save for the odd jar or two of pickled vegetables. Fortunately, I ate a hearty breakfast at an inn before casting off with Wharton, which, along with the meager provisions I carried in my bag, should be enough to sustain me until tomorrow.

    I wandered over to a large picture window behind the davenport and stared out at the vast expanse of sea. The sun had come out, lifting the fog. The sea was calm, its sun-dappled surface at rest. But to the north an ominous stack of dark clouds caught my eye. A storm would be here by nightfall, if not sooner. I needed to get the lighthouse functioning before then.

    Without further delay, I carried my tools up the twisting stairwell to the lantern room. Like most lighthouses I'd visited over the years, this was a cramped, iron-framed space surrounded on three sides by thick panes of glass. It smelled of mildew and decay. The condition of the lantern was as I expected: the wick needed to be trimmed, the whale oil refilled, and the lantern panes cleaned inside and out.

    I set about at once to my duties. Fortunately, all the supplies I needed were well-stocked: oil, cleaning tools, additional lamps, and a vast array of brushes. The lamp was encased in a Fresnel lens of the sixth order called a *lanthorn*. I cleaned the lanthorn thoroughly until it sparkled. Satisfied, I then inspected the mechanism that burned the oil and pumped it up from a reservoir below by means of weighted clockworks. Salty sea air tended to erode the metalwork if not properly maintained, and I could see it was already taking its toll on the mechanism.

As I worked to clean the oil pump, I heard a noise near the bottom of the stairs. The floorboards creaked as though someone were pacing back and forth in the house. This was followed by the scraping sound of fingernails dragged across the walls, and then, the loud crash of a heavy object striking the floor.

My mouth turned dry as a sanding sponge, and my throat sealed up with dread. Remembering the shadow of a man I'd seen earlier crossing the lantern room, I reached into my toolbox for a hammer before going down to face the intruder.

I rushed down the steps and quickly scanned the living room. If someone had been there, he was gone now. Immediately I inspected the kitchen. Finding nothing amiss, I flew upstairs to the bedrooms.

I stood on the landing and listened. All was calm and quiet. A quick check of the two drafty bedrooms revealed nothing. No intruder.

Damn peculiar, I thought as I returned to the main floor. I was sure of what I'd heard, and that it was coming from inside the house.

I did another sweep of the house. It was then that I discovered what I'd missed the first time: the source of the crashing sound.

In the corner across from the hearth, a small wooden writing desk was toppled over. A ledger lay splayed open like a crushed bird under the desk.

I righted the desk and picked up the ledger. It was the former keeper's record of happenings at the lighthouse. Usually, these were mundane records of daily lighthouse duties. In this case, however, I was astounded by the detail, the meandering thoughts, and the vivid observations of the sea.

This ledger captured more than the day to day particulars of a lighthouse keeper's life.

It was a record of a descent into madness.

I returned to the lanthorn and finished my work expeditiously. More than once I glanced outside, expecting to see the mysterious intruder rowing away in my skiff, my one and only link to the mainland. It troubled my mind that I had no convincing explanation for the sounds I'd heard and the presence I'd felt earlier. I'd checked everywhere a man or even a small child could hide. I'd even inspected the island outside, looking behind every boulder and rock outcropping for the stranger's presence. Alas, I found nothing.

Once the work was finished and I had the lighthouse functioning properly, I prepared a simple meal, and then set about making a blazing fire in the hearth. It was well into the afternoon and approaching evening. The westering sun sank toward the sea, and the storm I'd spied earlier was beginning to darken the sky.

Though I was accustomed to the variability of Maine's weather in early spring, the penetrating cold I felt in the house unnerved me. An unseasonably bitter chill squirmed through every crack and crevice in the walls and seeped into my bones. It wasn't until I sank into the reading chair by the blazing fire and opened the ledger that I felt my first moment of comfort in my new home.

The book was less a ledger of daily duties and more a journal of sorts, scrawled in a shaky hand, and from the moment I began reading it, I was mesmerized. The old keeper's name was Saul Langston. He was married to a woman named Sarah and had two children, Thomas and Eve. They settled at the lighthouse last summer, and by all accounts seemed to be happy in their new surroundings, if not a little overwhelmed by the tempests thrown at them by the sea.

However, there were moments of bliss and contentment as well. Friends and relatives visited from the mainland. Birthday parties were thrown for the two children. Accounts of beautiful full moons, a lunar eclipse, and the Northern Lights were described in brilliant detail.

All seemed to be going well for the keeper and his family until things changed. The weather turned bitter cold and the Atlantic more aggressive. Winter's long string of gray and miserable weeks could corrode a man's soul, and it was during this time that Saul's writing became more erratic and he appeared ill at ease with the isolation on Shaw Island.

And then the stranger arrived.

Part of the duties of every lighthouse keeper was to watch the sea with a perceptive eye and help any sailor in need. Despite the beacon, every now and then inexperienced seafarers struck a shoal or ledge, and men needed rescuing from the sea. On one evening in late November, Saul wrote of a ship entering the harbor…

A winter storm was raging, and through the whipping snow I watched the clipper sway and teeter on the restless ocean. Next, a colossal wave came out of nowhere and struck the vessel on its starboard side, throwing men overboard and capsizing the vessel.

Over my wife's objections, I row my skiff out to where I'd seen the men fall overboard. When I arrived, I found the bodies of dead sailors floating like driftwood everywhere. I shuddered at the horror on the men's frozen faces as they gaped up at me from the black waters. Their deaths had been quick but not without pain. I called out for survivors, but nobody called back.

Despairing, he was about to turn back when a voice called to him above the howling wind. Relieved to find someone to help, Saul navigated his skiff across the sea of dead to a man waving desperately for help.

He was floating away from the others, as though he'd somehow gotten separated during the sinking.

Once he'd dragged the man on board and wrapped him in a blanket, he rowed at once back to Shaw Island. Each time his oar bumped a body, he said a silent prayer. He knew a proper Christian burial was not in any of these sailors' futures; instead, the Atlantic would be each man's cold, watery tomb.

The man whom Saul rescued stared at him with an odd expression. Saul found the man's intensity disconcerting, as well as the fact that he didn't shiver even once despite his soaked clothing and the frigid wind. His skin was mottled gray, blue around the fingertips and eyes, and his breaths came in in short, wheezy gasps. He looked dead already, in Saul's estimation, but the fact he still drew air spurred the old keeper to put his back into his rowing and get the young man to safety before the elements could claim him.

There was much more to Saul's tale, and while curiosity urged me to continue reading, I had to see to my evening lighthouse duties.

Dusk was rapidly approaching. The sky rumbled with thunder as I ascended the steps to the lantern room. A keeper's duty went beyond merely lighting the wick. In the evening, I needed to check wind direction and adjust the vents to allow just enough draft into the lantern room. This created the necessary vacuum to draw the fumes and soot up the glass chimney attached to the top of the lamp and out of the lantern room. Then, during the course of the evening, I would need to return to properly trim the wicks, clean the chimney, adjust the vents, and wind the weights once more.

Once the work was completed, I returned to the warmth of the fire. It took several minutes for the chill of the lighthouse to thaw. When at last I felt comfortable again, I returned to Saul's account of the mysterious shipwrecked stranger.

The sailor, who speaks not a single word to Sarah or me, sits on the davenport and stares bleakly into the fire. He takes a few sips of broth but appears to neither care for the taste nor the comfort of the food. Despite the heat of the fire, which I stoke to a roaring blaze, the stranger's pale skin remains stippled with blue. I catch Sarah more than once out of the corner of my eye crossing herself as she keeps her distance from our strange guest.

Then she lets out a scream. The stranger has stood from the davenport and is moving toward the window. His eyes: dead and black, fascinated by what he sees out in the darkness. But what causes Sarah's distress is the knife in his hand, a long steel blade he must have produced from an inner coat pocket.

The stranger looks down at it like he's never seen it before, and then rests his empty gaze on me. He raises his arm and offers the knife to me with pleading eyes. "I...I cannot do it anymore," he says oddly. Emotion clouds his face, and it appears he is going to cry.

I quickly snatch the weapon from his hand. It is icy cold. Stunned, I drop it with a clatter and kick it out of the way. The stranger *has turned back to study the winter storm again, his expression filled with relief, as if a burden had been lifted from him. I urge Sarah to take Thomas and Eve up to their bedrooms and wait for me there. I need a word alone with the creature.*

I shuddered as I read the last line. To refer to a man as a "creature" was most unsettling and spoke to Saul's great fear. During my time on the *U.S.S. Chesapeake* I'd seen men in shock who'd fallen overboard, but at no point did I feel like they'd lost their humanity and were a threat to others. What innate influences did Saul receive from this man to warrant such a reaction?

My own discomfort grew when I felt the weight of eyes upon the back of my neck. I glanced over my shoulder more than once, expecting to find someone standing in the shadows of the lighthouse stairwell.

No one, of course, was there.

A sudden blast of wind struck the house. The ocean began to roar outside; waves crashed like cannon balls against the island. I knew I should check the lanthorn to make sure the wick was still lit, but I was too riveted to my chair and the warmth of the fire to move.

And too concerned with Saul's predicament to close his story just yet.

I continued to read as the storm wailed outside. A day had now passed, and still the nameless sailor brooded restlessly by the fire. And his physical condition deteriorated rapidly. He was losing weight. His skin had turned sallow, almost translucent, and stunk like a beached whale carcass. The steel blue of his eyes turned the same shade of gray as the sea.

The man would answer questions with only monosyllables and grunts. He apparently would not speak of the knife or the circumstances of the shipwreck no matter how many times Saul pushed him.

His continued presence in the house affected the mood of the whole family. Saul admitted to his own growing fascination with the knife, pondering the nicks and scratches on its curved serrated blade. The children would hide in their rooms, afraid to come out and face the stranger. And Sarah even confided to Saul her regrets that the stranger hadn't gone down with the rest of the shipwrecked crew.

Saul would hear none of it, however. It was his duty as keeper to save lives as well as keep the wick burning. He would care for this man, no matter how odd his mannerisms, until he was well enough to go home.

But when would that be? Sarah begged.

I appreciated Saul's sense of duty and honor; yet he seemed to be obsessing over the stranger. What hold did their mysterious guest have over Saul's mind?

Judging by the last journal entry, Saul's mental state was growing increasingly erratic. And violent. Perhaps he realized too late the toll his duty was exacting.

I know what madness feels like now. Its creeping sensation through the body, its strength in the limbs. I stare at the knife all day as if driven to pick it up and use it for, for its intended purpose. What purpose could that be? What does the creature want of me? Why won't it SPEAK to me of the knife, for God's sake!

I am sure he doesn't breathe. I watch as he sits by the window staring out at the sea all day. A seeping chill rests upon the room, as if I've brought into my home a thing long dead and not of this world. When he turns his eyes to me, it is as if I'm being given a command. I look to the knife every time.

The knife.

It rests on the mantel.

I know what I must do but I resist, I resist with all my will, but the calling is too great. I pick it up, weigh it in my hand, flex my fingers around its hilt, and call for my lovely family

The last sentence ended abruptly, the letters streaking down the page as if his hand had grown too weary to hold the pen anymore. I was left with the chilling certainty that I had just read the final thoughts of a murderer.

Relieved to have something to do to occupy my mind, I prepared to attend to my duties in the lighthouse when a glint of light caught my eye.

There, sitting on the mantel, was the knife described in Saul's journal. How had I missed it earlier? Bewildered, I couldn't take my eyes off it. It was waiting…but for what? I had no idea. I just knew it was *meant* for me to find it.

My heart pounding madly, I picked the knife up carefully and examined it from all angles, recalling Wharton's words from earlier:

The last keeper even went mad and attacked his own family. Blood was found on the walls and floor of every room, as if he hunted them down like prey. When it was over, he threw himself from the top of the lighthouse. But his wife and children...they weren't so lucky, sir. Their death was slow and brutal.

I saw it all as Wharton described, in a tableau of grisly images racing through my mind:

The children's bodies bloodied and crumpled in the corner of their bedroom...

Sarah, pressing her hands against the wound in her stomach, blood leaking around her fingers, as her husband came up behind her and shoved her down the stairs, her neck snapping like a dry twig at the bottom...

Saul, blood-stained hands trembling, climbing the stairs to the lantern room...

I screamed and dropped the knife. It clattered on the floor, and at that same moment I heard a loud bang upstairs. Startled, I looked up in time to see a shadow glide along the stairs.

An impulse to flee overwhelmed me, but I held fast and waited for it to pass. I needed to confront the horror residing in this house. This was *my* home now, and reason and logic dictated that everything I'd seen and heard up until now was impossible, an anomaly of the senses. I steeled myself for what I might discover in the upper rooms, and though my body quaked, I scooped up the knife and climbed the stairs slowly, keeping alert for any sign of the intruder.

When I reached the landing, I was struck by an unsettling cold. A rank odor filled the house: briny sea air mixed with rotting flesh. Shivering, I pressed ahead to the open door at the end of the hall. To my great surprise and horror, a ghastly apparition stood before the wide-open window, gazing out at the storm-tossed sea!

It turned to me as I walked in. I recognized the apparition at once as the "creature" Saul described in his journal. He wore a midshipman's uniform of first lieutenant rank: a blue navy frock coat, white lace around the sleeves, and a band of white around the top of the coat. The sailor looked to be no older than twenty, though his corpse-like, sickly pallor, made him appear ancient. His eyes were black as inkwells, and they fixed on the knife I held out before me with loathing.

My fear of the apparition quickly diminished at that moment. His suffering was evident, and I wanted nothing more than to help.

"Who are you?" I asked.

By all accounts, I expected no answer, but suddenly the apparition frowned, and the words he spoke were twisted with pain.

"It wasn't meant to happen this way," he said, turning back to the window.

"What wasn't?" I edged closer to him. "Tell me, so I may help you."

He heaved a heavy sigh. "So much killing," he said, shaking his head.

I followed his gaze out the window and saw, to my astonishment, the dark outline of a small ship floundering on the raging sea. I could tell by its aft and fore sails and single mast that it was a sloop, and I thought I could make out in the bursts of lightning the outlines of six cannons mounted on her deck.

Was it even there? Or was I imaging this as well, like I did the deaths of Saul and his family when I held the knife downstairs?

I waited and watched as the ocean battered the small seafaring vessel until its rigging broke apart and its mast collapsed. Something felt wrong to me, however. I thought of Saul's account of the sinking ship. He described it as a clipper, an entirely different class of ship. What, then, was I witnessing now?

"We went down in the storm that night," the phantom continued, as if sensing my bewilderment. "Pirates boarded our vessel just before the storm hit, killing our officers and throwing their bodies out to sea. We never saw the attack coming. So much killing," he repeated.

"You mean, you…"

He turned to look at me. "There were no survivors."

I took a step away. "But Saul, he rescued you…"

The apparition's expression hardened, and his eyes dropped to the knife in my hand. "They sliced the captain's throat open and cut the hands off anyone who got in their way. I tried to stop them. I grabbed the knife and wrestled it away from them, but I was overpowered. They tossed me overboard. Then ... then..."

Utter confusion wracked the tormented spirit's face.

"Saul rescued you," I said, "only he thought you were part of the crew of the sinking clipper."

"I was still so angry."

I nodded with understanding. "You didn't mean for Saul's family to die. But your rage at your own death infected him, and he—" I couldn't finish the sentence. I thought of Saul's volatile state of mind. How the weather and the island were already chiseling away at his sanity before the night of the shipwreck. He must have been already one step away from murder...

The apparition's grim features softened. "What year?" he asked.

"1869," I told him.

The apparition hung his head. "Ten long years at the bottom of the sea."

"What can I do?" I asked.

Again, his eyes flicked to the knife. "Throw it away or I shall never find peace."

I understood at once. Without further delay, I left the lighthouse and walked out to the edge of the island. I waited for the right moment and flung the knife as far as I could into the sea. With the task completed, I returned to the house to assure the dead sailor that all had been set right again, but to my disappointment I found the apparition had vanished. The chill in the air and the foul odor were gone too, and the house felt empty again.

I stood at the window where the spirit had been and watched the waves crash against the rocks below, pondering what Wharton had said about how the sea had a way of dragging men down.

It would seem, on occasion, it could dredge them up, too.

I'LL RETURN FOR YOU

He wasn't there when she died, but he should have been. Maybe the accident never would have happened if he hadn't begged off going on the trip to visit his wife's parents. Tight deadlines for work had put pressure on him to stay home and finish an already overdue project.

So he let his wife drive alone, in a storm, in her junky car with bald tires and bad transmission. He tried to offer her his pick-up truck, but she wouldn't hear of it. She liked her little Mazda, the same car she'd driven since college, and felt more comfortable driving it than his road hog of a vehicle. He regretted letting her win the argument, regretted it with an increasingly sharp pang of guilt with each passing day.

The worst had come to pass. The sheer cliff on the side of the narrow mountain road was at least sixty feet high, with ocean eddies and jagged rocks waiting at the bottom. It was dark, the rain a curtain of silver that the headlights could barely penetrate, and she didn't know the way. Didn't realize how sharp the bend in the road was, either. There should have been a guardrail, but local officials didn't allow one. The plows had to clear the road during the wintertime.

It was over in seconds, according to the coroner's report. Official cause of death was listed as drowning. But blunt force trauma may have knocked her unconscious and saved her from too much suffering.

And just like that, a brightly shining candle full of promise was snuffed out in the world.

~⚓~

It was about a month after the accident that the nightmares began.

James would find himself in the passenger seat of a car driving along a dark road at night. Beside him sat Lynn, sweating, hunched over the steering wheel, squinting out into the storm. Ferocious wind and whipping rain made it nearly impossible to see anything but tatters of light.

Then, a sudden lurch as tires slipped on loose gravel, and momentum carried the car to the edge of the cliff. And over.

What came next was a flood of sounds and careening images as the little Mazda hatchback rolled down the mountainside: Lynn's screams filling the car's compartment with horror; his head striking the windshield, door, and dashboard almost at once; his body tossing about like flotsam on an ocean current, each blow a white-hot burst of pain as blood vessels erupted and bones shattered into pieces.

Then the car struck the water with a thunderous splash. The sounds of twisting and tearing metal was replaced with a hushed gurgle as the car sank quickly into the ocean.

And in all the dreams Lynn looked the same. Her head lay on its side against the steering wheel, one eye bruised shut, the other open and staring at him. If there had been accusation in that eye he couldn't have blamed her; but instead there was only sorrow and a lifetime's worth of regret mixed with horror and shock. Her lower lip quivered as her mouth formed an O in an obvious struggle for speech.

"Don't speak," he heard himself say, but a slight shake of her head told him to listen.

"I'll return for you, James. And we'll be together ... forever."

The briny ocean water rose to her chin and lips. Within moments it leaked into her mouth and then flooded her lungs. Her body shuddered with spasms, and plumes of dark red blood clouded the colorless water around her mouth. And then she was still.

Comforted by the dark.

When he awoke, his heart was jackhammering, and his arms and legs were flailing as though he were still in the car, sinking into the sea.

Sobbing, he lay in bed looking up at the ceiling, calling Lynn's name over and over. When after several minutes he caught his breath and had control over his emotions, he glanced at the clock next to his bed. Sunrise was less than an hour away. Birds were already chirping in the trees outside his window. The long shadows of a setting full moon fell into his room.

When it became apparent that sleep had abandoned him, James rose from bed and decided to go for a walk. Moonlit strolls were his and Lynn's favorite thing to do when they couldn't sleep, when the stresses of job and family took their toll.

Their house was never going to be big enough for all the children they'd been planning to have, but it had many charming features, including the patch of woodland behind their backyard that hid plenty of scenic trails. Their favorite one emerged onto a small cove, where James and Lynn used to like to sit and look out over the water on warm summer evenings and imagine their future children running and jumping off the end of the dock.

Before going outside, James stopped at one of the bedrooms and opened the door. Under the window sat the crib where their son Tyler slept, bathed in moonlight. James approached the crib and looked down at the smooth white linen lining the mattress.

Empty.

As it was last night.

As it had been for over a year.

He reached down and touched the spot where his son used to lay, his little pink face gazing up at him in his tiny blue cocoon. He remembered the gurgling coos and the random smiles. The sweet laughter. And the way his son's blue eyes flared with curiosity whenever James played magic tricks with his toys.

He remembered each and every day of Tyler's short three-month life with an almost uncanny clarity. The memories were woven into his every waking moment, and each memory brought into stark relief the emptiness of his current life. He couldn't go a day, an hour, even a minute without thinking of his wife's relentless optimism for the future and his son's bright-eyed joy at living. His solitude echoed with their haunting voices, the memories of which held him in an urgent, needy grip. Memories that were beacons of another life, another world, a world he felt more connected to than the one he lived in now.

With a heavy sigh, he turned away from Tyler's crib and left his room. Left it to the ghosts of ancestors to mourn the child and debate what could have been. He could almost sense their disapproval as he closed the door with a soft click and lumbered down the hallway.

In the kitchen, he put his shoes and coat on and walked outside.

The morning air was cool and refreshing, drying the sweat on his face and neck instantly, but the jitters remained from his terrifying dream, and he was unable to get out of his mind the image of Lynn's dying gaze.

After a few minutes of brisk walking he started to feel better. The narrow path was a ribbon of darkness winding through moon-glazed trees, but he knew it well enough to avoid the roots and jutting rocks that threatened to twist hikers' ankles.

When he came out on the other side, the cove was quiet and still. Insects hummed faintly in the tall grass. The soft pink of dawn blushed in the east. He gazed at the smooth, silver surface of the water and almost didn't recognize the grim figure that stared back, with its deep pockets of exhaustion around the eyes and anguish etched into its face.

A large rock outcropping made an ideal place to sit and contemplate the water. It was here, in the spot where he'd spent countless days with Lynn talking over their future, that he pondered his inexplicable fate.

None of it seemed real—none of it. His loneliness was a thing that pressed on his chest and squeezed his heart. How could he have been away so much from his family when they needed him the most? His friends assured him that none of it was his fault; his doctor told him the same as he wrote prescriptions for his relief. The words and the medicine did little to diminish the pain, however. When he closed his eyes, the memories of the night Tyler died were always there waiting for him.

James, I'm at the hospital. You need to come home now. Something is wrong with Tyler.

Away with his team at a conference in Boston. Knocking back drinks at the hotel bar.

I don't know what to do, James. He's stopped breathing. They can't bring him back.

The voice message already three hours old.

The next flight wasn't until six o'clock the next morning. By the time he arrived home he found Lynn crumpled on the couch, crying hysterically, surrounded by her sister and parents. Tyler was gone. He stayed up with her the rest of the night, consoling her, until she collapsed into a restless sleep in his arms.

For the next several weeks a bitter tension grew between them, one that lingered under the surface of every quiet moment they spent together. James didn't want to poke at it, didn't want to expose it to the light. Tyler's death was an open wound he couldn't bear to touch. He grew up watching his parents and the long intervals of silence between them, and learned some things were best kept in the dark.

Starved of the attention they crave, some problems will wither into dust until time sweeps them away.

James hoped he was right, and the wound their relationship suffered would heal. As the months went by, the tension between them began to improve. Their easy laughter returned. Moments like walks in the woods didn't seem so forced, so contrived to bring normalcy back into their lives. Instead, it felt like the natural rhythms and routines of their old lives had returned.

It felt, to James at least, that there was hope for a new beginning. The possibility of restarting their family again. And Lynn confided that she felt the same.

And so life began to return to normal.

Until the accident.

James watched the smooth unbroken surface of the bay begin to ripple and bubble. He knew black sea bass, bullheads and trout roamed the dark nether regions of the harbor. He'd fished for them himself many times before. Having grown up around water, he was accustomed to all the sights and sounds of the cove.

Except the one he was seeing now out in the middle of the bay.

Something large and metallic bobbed gently on the waves. It was squarish in shape with a rounded top, moonlight glinting off shiny glass. He walked to the end of the dock to get a closer look.

His breath caught in his throat.

It was a car.

Its sudden appearance startled him, but before he could think about what it was doing there and where it had come from, he flung off his shoes and jacket and dived into the water.

James.

He sliced through the chilly water with long, powerful strokes reminiscent of his old varsity swimming days. His heart throbbed in his ears; his breath was quick and raspy. He was only twenty feet away when he heard a soft voice slice whisper:

James, I returned for you.

I returned.

He reached the car and tried to open the door, but the water pressure kept it shut. He wiped the mist away from the glass and looked inside the compartment. It was filling up fast, and the car was sinking into the murky depths too quickly for him to do anything.

But he had to try. Because she was there. Lynn. Crushed behind the wheel, her expression frozen in shock and terror.

I told you I'd come back.

And then her body shuddered, and her head lifted off the steering wheel. In that moment it was as if a veil lifted, and she returned to him, glowing with warmth and life. Her broken teeth were whole again, her bruises healed. Her eyes, previously swollen shut, beamed love for him. Her smile was the sweetest thing, bringing tears to his eyes.

The car sank but he held on to its twisted frame, fixated on his wife's loving gaze.

Oh, James…

The water lapped at his mouth and nose. He saw her twist slightly and there, in her arms, was a bundle that squirmed and cried. The baby looked at James with sudden recognition, its blue eyes flashing love.

The crying stopped.

The chill of the bay's waters embraced James, and he sank gratefully into it, with his wife and child.

His life complete.

LEECHES

WITH OLIVIA ANN SMITH

Summer of 2019

It was a hot August day, the kind you remember as a kid lasting forever. A day of endless blue skies, of dreams with no end, of humming insects, soft breezes perfumed with wildflowers, and a barbecue to look forward to in the backyard that evening.

And it was a great day for a swim.

Squealing with delight, Ellie ran out of the house to the family's pond. The oval-shaped pond glistened in the sunlight, buzzed with the rapid whirring of dragonflies on patrol. Ellie backed up and got ready to cannonball. She started running, jumped as high as she could, and came down with a *splash* in the water. She swam around for several minutes, enjoying the cool water, when she felt a sharp pain on the bottom of her foot. Something stuck to her. She started kicking wildly to get it off, but the pain worsened, shooting up her leg. She felt another spike of pain, and she imagined a needle-like proboscis probing under her skin. She started to scream. Water immediately rushed into her mouth. She choked and flailed some more, and that's when she noticed dozens of little slimy blobs all over her arms and legs, pulling her down. They injected thick black ooze into her body.

 Ellie started to feel dizzy. She knew she was going to die.

 Ellie stared out the car window and watched the trees whiz by. She rolled the window down and stuck her head out like a dog. She loved feeling the breeze…hot but refreshing! Ellie's mom grabbed her arm and pulled her back into the car. Ellie's little brother, Bobby, started kicking the back of her seat.

 "Stop it, Bobby!" Ellie cried.

 Mom turned around and tapped him on the leg. Bobby knew what it meant and stopped kicking. Ellie took her iPhone and earbuds out of her backpack and slipped them on. She put on some rock music, sat back, and looked out the window.

A few hours later Mom pulled into the driveway of their new home in Connecticut. Excited, Ellie flung her door open and jumped out, but her legs almost buckled beneath her. She hadn't walked for hours. She steadied herself and walked up to the house. It was a huge, three-story house, painted white, with black shutters and a bright red door.

Slinging her backpack over her shoulder, Ellie followed her mom inside. Together, they explored their new home, which Ellie had to admit was about three times the size of their little house back in Ohio. The only thing she'd miss about Ohio was her father, who stayed behind to wrap up loose ends at work. She wouldn't miss most of the other kids at her old school. They just didn't understand her. And they were mean, besides.

Once she chose her new bedroom and put her things down on the bed, she wandered over to the window. The backyard was vast and emerald-green, and in the middle of it sat a pond.

The pond from my dream, she thought with a tiny shiver.

Lovely and idyllic, it sat invitingly and waited for children to splash in its cool waters. Ellie loved the Laura Ingalls Wilder books, and she pretended now that she was Laura, having one of her simple adventures.

A pond in my own backyard. How did I get so lucky?

She grinned as she turned away from the window and raced back down the stairs.

Let's go find some adventure, she thought.

In the still air the pond lay like a huge silver mirror on the ground. In its reflection she saw her freckles, the dimple in her chin, and the blue ribbons she wore in her hair. The girl in the pond looked happy, but how did she really feel about her new home? Only time would tell, she guessed.

Tall grasses stuck out in various places around the pond's shore. An occasional insect skittered across its surface. Ellie found a long stick and used it to poke the bottom, watching little eddies of mud circle around. Then she heard a grinding sound. Ellie took the stick out. A huge bite was taken out of it! Frightened, she threw the stick in the water and ran back to the house.

"Mom, mom!" Ellie cried as she stomped into the kitchen. "There's a monster in the pond!"

"Don't be silly, dear," her mother replied, stacking cans of soup in the cupboard.

"Ooh, monster! I want to see!" Bobby cried, disappearing out the door into the backyard.

"Bobby, wait!"

Her little brother was about to jump into the pond when Ellie tackled him from behind. She carried him under his arms, kicking and screaming, back into the house.

"Ellie, put your little brother down," Mom said. "What has gotten into you?"

"Mom, you've got to believe me," Ellie pleaded. "There's a monster in the pond!"

"What are you talking about?"

Ellie told her about the grinding sounds and the stick that had bites taken out of it.

"Could be anything," her mom declared, one hand on her hip and the other wagging a finger at Ellie. "We probably have a big hungry fish on our property who thought you were offering him a tasty snack. Now go on upstairs and wash up for dinner—and leave your little brother alone!"

Sighing, Ellie did as she was told, but she kept an eye on Bobby to make sure he didn't try to bolt out the door and back to the pond. Mom was probably right. Most likely, it was just a stupid fish and not a monster.

As she scrubbed her hands in the bathroom sink, she started giggling to herself. A monster...what a crazy idea! Maybe she should stop watching so many horror movies with Dad.

That was the answer. Horror movies.

And a highly active imagination.

The next day Ellie wanted to make it up to her mother. She knocked on Bobby's door and asked him to help her clean the house. She could hear him now: *The house is so BIG, Ellie, and it will take all day!* But she wouldn't take no for an answer. Mom deserved it after that long drive from Ohio to Connecticut.

When she didn't receive an answer, Ellie opened the door. To her surprise, Bobby was gone. She checked the rest of the house, but he was nowhere to be found. Then a horrible thought struck her. She flew to one of the back windows that looked over the pond.

Thank goodness he isn't there, she thought.

Ellie found her mother upstairs folding laundry. "Mom, where is Bobby?" she asked.

"I don't know," she answered. "I thought he was with you."

"He's not."

Mom frowned. "Where could he be?"

They searched everywhere, both inside and all over the grounds, calling his name until their voices turned hoarse. Finally, Mom ran to the phone and dialed 911.

She told them what happened. Soon enough the police arrived. They searched the grounds but found nothing. One of the detectives named Grady stayed behind after the search to talk to Ellie's mother. Ellie was shooed out of the room so the adults could have privacy, but she sat at the bottom of the stairs, listening.

All the advice and recommendations. All the comfort and promises that the police would do everything to find Bobby. All the hope for a happy ending. All of it led to nothing. Days turned into weeks, with no sign of Bobby. The disappearance was a mystery. Eventually, after several more months of fruitless searching, the case was closed. The police moved on, and the nice detective who sat with her mother that first day stopped calling.

The reality of the situation struck Ellie like a hammer: Bobby wasn't coming home. Ever.

A year went by. Once in a while some of the neighbors would mount a half-hearted search of the nearby woods for clues to Bobby's disappearance, but nothing ever turned up. Ellie had learned not to get excited when new searches happened. No clues were waiting to be found. If it weren't for his still un-packed bedroom and the photographs that her mom put up all over the house, Ellie might have forgotten that Bobby even existed in the first place. He was just *gone*, like a mirage that vanishes when you get too close.

Her mother was quickly disappearing from Ellie's life, too. She was always in her bedroom. Her room was next to Ellie's, and at night she could hear her crying. It broke Ellie's heart. Sometimes she couldn't help but cry, too.

Mom never saw her. Ellie only crossed paths with her mother when she came out to make food for them, and even that wasn't every day. Then her mother would return straight to her bedroom, locking the rest of the world out.

It was a hot August day and a great time for a swim.

Squealing with delight, Ellie ran out of the house to the family's pond. The oval-shaped pond glistened in the sunlight, buzzed with the rapid whirring of dragonflies on patrol. Ellie backed up and got ready to cannonball. She started running, jumped as high as she could, and came down with a splash in the water. She swam around for several minutes, enjoying the cool water, when she felt a sharp pain on the bottom of her foot. She started kicking wildly to get it off her, but the pain worsened, shooting up her leg.

The thing, the *creature*, whatever it was, stuck tighter. She felt another spike of pain, and she imagined a needle-like proboscis probing under her skin. She started to scream. Water immediately rushed into her mouth. She choked and flailed some more, and that's when she noticed dozens of little slimy blobs all over her arms and legs, pulling her under. They injected thick black ooze into her body.

Leeches. Ellie started to feel dizzy. She knew she was going to die.

The leech that held tight to her leg grew bigger and bigger. Then she heard a voice bubbling up from the creature:

"Run, Ellie! Get away! If you get eaten, you will never come out!"

It was Bobby's voice! Bobby was inside the slimy black thing.

She flailed and fought against it, but the massive leech clamped tighter around her ankle. She could feel the cold slime of its throat oozing up her calf as its greedy mouth hungrily devoured her.

"I'm sorry, Ellie." Bobby's voice again, fading. *"I didn't mean for any of this to happen."*

Driven by terror, Ellie gave the thing a brutal kick to the face. It made a whimpering noise and loosened its grip on her. With great effort, Ellie was able to pull her leg out of its mouth and swim away. The giant leech gave her one last longing look before it darted away into the pond's murky depths. Its body was sleek, black, and elongated, its head bulbous like a doorknob, its mouth wide and filled with razor-sharp teeth. Ellie screamed when she emerged from the water and swam to shore. She couldn't stop screaming even when she was safe on land. The wound to her leg was bleeding badly and probably infected, so she ran back to the house, screaming for her mother. Once in the house, she closed and locked the door.

Her heart beating wildly, she raced to her mother's room, but the door was locked. Ellie glanced out a window in the hallway and saw the big black leech sliding and slipping toward the house. Thick, black ooze trailed behind it…no, not *it*. Bobby.

Her brother was heading straight to their mother's bedroom window! She pounded on her door, but the only answer she got was her mother's tired voice saying, "Go away, Ellie. I'm trying to sleep."

"Get out, Mom! Get out of the room—Bobby's coming to get you!"

Ellie shuddered in horror when she heard her mother's bedroom window shatter, followed by slurping and gargling sounds and her mother's terrified screams. It lasted for several seconds, seconds in which Ellie envisioned the worst possible fate for her mother. What would she become now? Would she be like Bobby, turned into a hideous monster?

After a few moments, everything became still and quiet.

Ellie ran to her room and locked the door. She knew she was next! She cowered under her sheets and blanket, closed her eyes like she used to when she was a little girl, and wished for it all to go away. For Bobby to go away. For the whole house, and Connecticut, and the pond to go away.

Her door squealed as something came in.

"Oh, *Ellie*." Her mother's voice, wet and gurgling. "Magical thinking won't save you now. Why don't you join us for a swim?"

Ellie screamed. And she didn't stop screaming until she was reunited with her whole family, at the bottom of the pond.

ONE WINTER NIGHT

The footsteps were getting closer. They skimmed through drifts of snow blown across the path, following him through the woods.

The man turned and looked. He saw only tree limbs encased in ice and snow, pointing wickedly in his direction. He was afraid of the darkness he'd find at the end of the path, but he couldn't go home yet.

The sorrow was too unbearable.

The wind was a vicious slap in the face, howling in his ears and raking his eyes with bitter claws. Yet he was beyond feeling now.

All around him the woods creaked like a rope hanging from an attic rafter. A noose, to be precise. When he closed his eyes, he saw the body swaying in the night air, the glassy, sightless eyes fixed on him. A vision seared into his memory forever.

He stopped to rest. Between his ragged breaths he thought he heard the footsteps on the path behind him, getting closer. It may have been an animal scurrying to its den, but he knew better.

The man massaged his throat, imagining the tautness of the rope around his lover's neck, the burning pain and pressure. The delivery by one's own hand into the abyss. He shuddered at the horror.

He understood solitude. He'd lived with it for ten long years now, never once failing to make this trek through the woods to the gravesite of his beloved wife on the anniversary of her death. He felt like fog passing through the darkness most days, insubstantial, waiting to move on himself, to be guided down a new path.

The man lurched forward without a sound and staggered through the woods. He had to narrow his eyes to pierce the darkness and see ahead to the clearing in the woods.

In the clearing sat a large and stately cemetery surrounded on all sides by a wrought iron fence, centuries old and hidden away from the prying eyes of outsiders. It served as the final resting place for the wealthy recluses who populated the nearby town. Even with all his money, which in an earlier time he regarded as merely material to waste, he could not find peace. He missed his wife too much.

As the voluntary caretaker of the cemetery, he had a key. After gaining entrance, he searched the rows of limestone monuments until he found the one he sought. On its rose-colored surface was carved a simple inscription, a Walter Savage Landor poem: Death stands before me, whispering low / I know not what into my ear; / Of his strange language all I know / Is, there is not a word of fear.

He had chosen it himself, hoping the words would bring him comfort. They had not.

A tree branch rattled behind him, and a woman appeared on the path he'd followed. In the moonlight, her pale skin glowed like a weak lamp, and her hair, the long, red locks of it he longed to touch again, tumbled down her shoulders and back.

She drifted closer to him. He raised his hand, begging her to take it, knowing, even as his heart swarmed with emotion, that she could not see him. He was dead to her, as dead as the barren forest in the grip of winter, as dead as the tenants who lie buried beneath his feet.

The woman's face crumpled into silent tears. The wind, when it breathed, did not stir her hair. She looked up at the sky, and the man, seeing the raw, swollen wound around his wife's slender neck, called her name.

"Clarissa!"

But the vision he waited for every year vanished, scattered by the wind and snow, leaving only the sorrow and darkness he would live with for another year.

THE MIDNIGHT CHARIOT

This story has been told many times over the ages. Now it shall be told once more, for those who have forgotten its lessons.

Princess Luna lived with her family in a gleaming castle high above the tiny hamlet of Nightville. Luna was the younger of two sisters, and at fourteen, also the most disobedient. She was a petty girl, who spent long hours staring at her plain face in the palace mirror, and daydreaming about love, glory, and riches. She was also bitterly jealous of her older sister, the lovely and graceful Princess Olivia, who was due to be wed in a fortnight.

One evening Luna stood outside her sister's bedchamber. She listened as her mother described Olivia's upcoming wedding.

"It will be so *lovely*," boasted the Queen. "Thousands of roses, dahlias, and hydrangeas will transform our courtyard into a garden paradise. The finest minstrels and musicians from all over the land will entertain us. All the kings and queens from the Seven Kingdoms will be in attendance, and your stunning beauty will mesmerize them."

When Luna heard this, her rage—well-known around the kingdom—boiled.

She stormed away and returned to her own bedchamber. She spent the rest of the evening plotting her revenge.

Since the beginning, Luna's mother and father clearly favored Olivia. Olivia had the sort of beauty that stopped conversation when she walked into a room. Her eyes sparkled like sapphires and her smile made strangers forget what they were going to say.

By contrast, Luna was a forgettable sort of pretty. With her smattering of freckles, brown eyes, and intensely shy personality, she was easy to overlook. No matter how many Latin texts she memorized or stallions she learned to ride, Luna failed to impress her royal parents. Their lives revolved around Olivia. Nothing would ever change that fact.

As she lay in bed brooding and scheming, a knock came at her door. "May I come in?" she heard Olivia ask.

"What do you want?" grumbled Luna.

Olivia slowly opened the door. "I came to see if you were all right," she said. She stood in the threshold, clearly feeling unwanted. "Ever since I announced my marriage plans to Prince Randolph, you've been so distant around me. I want you to be happy, that is all."

Luna rolled over in her bed and glared at her. "You really want to make me happy?"

Her sister nodded. "More than anything!"

"Then you'll get out and leave me alone forever. You think you're so special, marrying a prince and all, but you'll see. Someday, very soon, I'll be the one everyone is talking about. My beauty will light up this world and no one will forget who I am!"

"One day, Luna, you will find the prince of your dreams, too."

Luna scoffed. "He will probably be a toad of a man and his castle half the size of Randolph's."

Princess Olivia looked stricken. "I'm sorry you feel that way," she responded sadly, closing the door.

Yes, you will be sorry, thought Luna.

After night dropped its cloak upon the world and the stars salted the sky, Luna approached the Outer Gate. She ordered the startled guards—who rarely heard the demure princess speak—to lower the gate and fetch her horse. She was sure the answer to all her problems would be found in the Forest of Magic. And she would do whatever it took to convince the witch who lived there to help her.

Princess Luna mounted her steed and shot off for the forest. After several minutes of hard riding through the near pitch-black woods, she paused to let the horse rest. All around her she heard the flutter of bats, the croaking of toads, and the whine of insects. She wished she'd thought to bring a lantern. With no light from above but the faint glimmer of stars, Luna could barely see her hands in front of her face.

Suddenly, her heartbeat spiked when she heard what sounded like singing coming from up ahead. Only it wasn't a tune that a traveling minstrel might sing; it was the screechy voice of the old crone Mystia, who resided in the heart of the forest.

As Luna came closer to the singing, she stopped and dismounted. Through the thickets, Luna spied the witch hunched over a cooking fire, a wooden spoon held inches from her mouth, about to taste the broth. But the old woman didn't move; she stared directly at Luna.

"Come out of the cold, my pretty one, and sit by the fire," purred the witch.

Luna approached cautiously and sat down across from Mystia.

"To what do I owe the honor of this royal visit?"

"I think you already know," said Luna, whose inclination was to get right to the point.

"Indeed, I do." The witch stirred her thickening broth slowly. The flickering firelight made the crags and scars of her stony face look like deep canyons. "These rheumy eyes of mine still have the Sight. I've watched you and your sister grow up, Princess Luna. Her beauty is well known throughout the land, as is your temper and impudence."

"I don't have time for a lecture from you, old woman. I need a magic spell. Give it to me, or I shall have your miserable cottage burned to the ground by my huntsmen!"

The witch's gaze blackened. "What is it your heart desires, my Lady?"

Luna looked the witch in the eye. "My parents do not notice me! They love Olivia more than life itself. I am like a ghost to them—or perhaps a regret. I want them to see *me* for who I am and love me as they do my sister!" She swiped at a tear that slid down her cheek.

The old witch smiled.

"As you wish, my dear. I have observed how you've lived your life in your sister's shadow, and what a burden it must be! With only a palace to spend your days in, and servants to wait on your every need, you are clearly a damsel in distress. I shall mix a potion for you at once. Wait right here."

The witch shuffled away into her cottage, leaving Luna to wait out in the cold. When the old hag returned several minutes later, she was holding a small cup. Wisps of steam rose from the liquid within. The revolting scent made Luna's nose wrinkle as she took it from the witch.

"It smells disgusting," she complained, as she brought it to her lips.

"Drink every drop, and then return to your chamber to sleep. When you awake in the morning, no one will look at you the same again."

Luna did as the old crone instructed, gagging on the dregs at the bottom. The flavor and consistency reminded her of seaweed she once ate on a dare when she was nine, only with the bitter aftertaste of coriander and wormwood. When she was finished, she dropped the cup to the ground, turned away from Luna without a word of thanks, and rode back to the castle. Upon reaching her chamber, she threw herself into bed and tried to ignore her complaining stomach.

Exhausted, she fell into a deep sleep.

When she awoke, the sun was a red blot of melted wax in the east. Eager to view the beauty that must be radiating from every pore in her skin, Luna dashed to the nearest mirror. But to her horror, she found the image that stared back at her to be more hideous than Mystia herself.

She screamed at the oozing sores and ugly black pock marks scattered across her face.

When her family heard her pitiful wailing, they burst into her chamber and cried out in alarm. "Oh, Luna," sobbed her mother, throwing her arms around her daughter. "What has happened to you? Who has done this to you?"

Luna choked back tears and said, "It was Mystia, the old crone of the woods. I went to visit her last night, and she cursed me! I was merely paying her a visit… and look what she's done!"

"What I did was exactly what Princess Luna demanded of me," a voice scolded. They turned to see Mystia lurch into the room and point her heavy oaken walking stick at Luna. "You wanted attention? Now I've given it to you, my pretty. See what jealousy gets you in the end."

"Release her from your curse, miserable old hag, or I shall have your head!" roared the King.

"Impossible, sire. Magic of this sort only travels one direction, you see. But I make you a proposal. I shall end your daughter's misery and at the same time teach a lesson to the people of Nightville. No longer shall the night be so dark and menacing. Your people shall have light to see by as they walk the straight and narrow. But should any of your subjects find themselves tempted to consort with black magic again, they need only look up at the blemished face of your daughter riding her midnight chariot to remind them of the consequences."

"Do it," begged Luna, "I cannot live this way!"

With the King's blessing, Mystia put Luna to sleep forever. Her face became the moon which emblazoned the night sky. All who gazed upon it said a silent prayer of gratitude and made sure to teach their children to avoid wickedness in all its forms.

The children listened, and Mystia was never seen or heard from again.

THE ROOT OF ALL EVIL

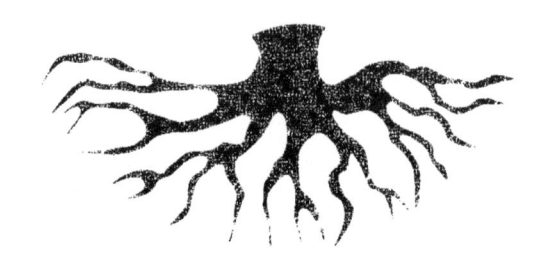

Ryan Hayes stood at the edge of the park, listening to the restless wind, his breath pluming in the cold autumn twilight. He peered into the gathering darkness and reflected on his old hometown and how much had changed in the past twenty years.

From what he could tell when he drove in that morning, not much, he thought grimly. Watson's Mill would always be the same old dreary town, stuck in the past with no future whatsoever. The same empty stores stood on Main Street with their fading, sunbaked facades. The house he grew up in sat wearily, waiting for time to grind it down into dust. The restaurants he ate in served the usual tasteless fare, and the faces who stared at him were as bland as he'd always remembered. People liked a distraction—he couldn't blame them for their curiosity—but at the same time he pitied them for living here on the edge of nowhere.

He was lucky he got out when he did; lucky he was able to make it in the publishing world and become something, before this insipid town could suck the best years out of his life like a thirsty vampire.

But not everyone was so fortunate.

He hurried across the park, past the swing sets and slides, past the sandbox where innocence still lingered like a sweet vapor in the air, and crossed over into a field. His feet slashing through dew-laden grass, he halted when he came to a small cluster of pine trees that formed a sort of wall. Beyond the trees stood a small, wooded area that he loved exploring as a kid with his friends.

He scanned the darkness, searching for the others. The ones he'd summoned.

"Thomas?" Ryan called. "Come out, come out, wherever you are."

"I'm here," answered a voice. A man emerged from the shadows, shivering and blowing on his hands.

Like the rest of the town, his best friend in high school hadn't changed much, except for maybe gaining a few extra pounds on top of his already substantial frame. He sported a beard thick enough to hide a squirrel in, and his beady eyes gleamed in the dark and studied Ryan with skepticism. "We all came back, like you asked. Now what are we doing here, Ryan?"

Ryan waited for the rest of them to step forward. From the shadows emerged Emma Gordon, the popular girl he first met in calc with the sparkling blue eyes and easy laugh. His first crush, truth be told. Beside her stood her hair-twirling and bubble gum-snapping friend Julie Mayfield, an awkward and insanely skinny girl in thick-framed glasses who moved to New York City after graduation to write for *Cosmo*. Last, he was pleased to see Elliot Newcomb, who crept up a little to stand behind Thomas, averting his eyes from Ryan's gaze. Nervous little Elliot, who dropped out of high school in the tenth grade and found work in an auto repair shop in the next town over. A loner whose idea of high living was a pint of Bud Lite and a poker game. Penny-ante, of course.

"Is Amy with you?" Ryan asked.

Emma shook her head sadly. "I couldn't get her out, Ryan. The staff at the institution say she's too weak and heavily sedated to have visitors, much less leave with anyone."

"You've been so good to her," Ryan answered distantly. "How are they treating her in there?"

"Like any state hospital."

"I see. Has she spoken since that day?"

"Not a word. If she makes any sound at all, it's usually crying or whimpering in a dream. The doctors say she's lost her mind."

Ryan frowned. "Your words or theirs?"

"Both."

Thomas shifted uncomfortably. "Why did you ask us to meet you here, Ryan?"

As if in response, a chilly gust of air, suggestive of an icy winter to come, rattled the branches.

"You'll soon see," Ryan told him. "It took a little time to track you all down—except for you, Thomas. Your big, burly picture is all over the news. Sort of like a hometown hero, I guess, with you running for governor and all. Besides, I thought you used to like the park. I seem to recall your fondness for the trees."

"Not anymore."

They followed Ryan into the wooded area, which, after a short walk, opened into a clearing. On the top of a small, rounded hill sat an oak tree of such immense size and sprawl that it seemed as though it were trying to embrace the whole earth. In the waning light of dusk, each branched looked like the gnarled fingers of an old man stricken with arthritis. The grotesquery of the tree made them each cringe as they remembered playing under it as children and carving their initials in its trunk, picnicking with their families in its cool, leafy shade, and climbing up its stout branches.

From the top you could see across Watson's Mill to the blue water tower on the other end of town. Each of them had taken a turn experiencing the breathtaking view, and none of them had forgotten the exultant feeling of being the tallest humans in the world at that precarious moment.

Now the tree was a mere shadow of what it once was. Clouds of black insects could be seen hovering over its hollowed-out limbs. Bats took off from its higher extremities and darted across the darkening sky, swooping ominously close to their heads. A smell, the apple-sweet stench of autumn rot, filled the air.

"It feels like…we're being watched," Emma said, shivering.

"Oh, c'mon, it's just a tree." Elliot pointed up to it. "Look at it. It looks like it's going to fall down on its own at any moment."

"So sad," breathed Julie's soft voice.

"You see the change," said Ryan.

"Of course we see it!" shouted Thomas. "I can't believe that diseased thing even still stands. I'd have thought by now someone would have cut it down, especially—"

"—after what happened?" Ryan finished for him. "Is that it, Thomas? Chop it down, say our final prayers, and then forget what happened to our friend here?"

"Look, Ryan, we know what Danny meant to you." Emma moved in front of him so she could look him in the eyes. "But this is really too much! I mean, what's the point of being here?"

"Why did you all come back?" Ryan demanded, scowling at each of them in turn. He ran his fingers through his black hair and gestured up at the tree. "You know what it's all about. I can't let you forget what he meant to us. When I came back last year and saw this disease eating away at the tree, I could tell something was wrong. I could almost hear him. Not as a cry but something much harsher, and it wasn't only directed at me. He wants to see all of us."

"Who?" Elliot asked.

"Danny."

"Danny's dead, Ryan." Julie's body shook as she said the somber words. "This is all in your head."

"Twenty years ago today," Ryan conceded, "and I know you think I'm crazy, but I'm not!"

"That's not what she means…" Emma reached out and touched his arm, but Ryan pushed her hand away.

"I'll show you," he said.

"What are you talking about?" Elliot asked.

"He's up there."

"On the hill?"

"In the tree."

Thomas laughed. "You *are* crazy."

"Then follow me."

"I'm not going up there."

"What are you afraid of, Thomas?"

"Ryan, stop. You're scaring me," Julie said, before Emma went over and gave her a hug.

"Everything scares you, Julie, and it always did!"

"Please, Ryan," Emma pleaded. "You've been bombarding us with texts, phone calls and e-mails for the past month, begging us to come here. We thought you wanted to meet us for dinner and drinks, talk about the old times, not re-enact some childish fantasy of yours."

"'Childish fantasy'?" Ryan fumed. "Danny is dead!"

"It was an accident, man." Thomas approached him slowly, his hands open placatingly. "There was nothing that could be done. The branch broke, he slipped…"

"No." Ryan shook his head.

"What do you mean?"

"That's not what I saw."

"That's what happened."

"I was *there*, Thomas, right next to him, climbing the tree, and I saw what it did to him."

"It?" Emma repeated, backing away slowly with Julie. "What the hell are you talking about?"

"You know damn well what I'm talking about."

"It's just a tree, Ryan."

"For a long time that's what I thought, Emma, but then something changed."

"No. You're wrong."

"Follow me and I'll show you."

"I don't want to."

"Why not?" Ryan's eyes blazed. "Because you know I'm right, is that it? Because deep down, you know the truth about how Danny died that day!"

Elliot shook his head. "We all saw it, man! The way his neck broke when he hit the ground."

"Then follow me."

Elliot scoffed. "This is nuts…"

"What do you have to lose?"

"All right," Thomas stepped forward and jabbed his finger at Ryan's chest. "We'll go, but only to humor you. We'll get a good close look at the tree, listen to what it has to say, and then we're getting the hell out of here!"

"And don't ever call us again," Elliot added, his eyes cold with conviction.

Ryan sighed with relief. "That's all I ask."

With loping strides, Ryan led the way up the slick hill. The others followed behind, occasionally slipping in the dewy grass. The cold tightened their legs, cramped their muscles. Sweat sheened their foreheads.

The tree, clearly hundreds of years old, was dying, its jagged limbs and chipped bark literally flaking like dead skin before their eyes. A squirrel scurried down the trunk and disappeared in the tall grass and weeds in which the tree stood silently.

Yet the tree seemed to welcome them, its outstretched branches like open arms wishing to embrace the children who'd come back for one last visit.

Ryan turned to the others. "Don't tell me you don't remember," he said, like an accusation.

No one argued. They paused to catch their breaths and replay that summer day from long ago.

A day filled with the promise of childhood adventures that became, in an instant, a lifetime of horrific memories.

In Danny's opinion, this was unthinkable.

He heard the buzzing but assumed it was something flying by overhead. In all his days of climbing trees and taunting danger, this had never happened before.

He had been careful to avoid the diseased branches and the ones that looked cracked and aged and possibly unable to support his weight. He wasn't a skinny kid like his friend Ryan, so he had to be careful about which foothold he placed his faith in.

But it was worth the danger. The view from the top of the tree was breathtaking. He could even see his own housetop and backyard. "Flirting with disaster," to quote his mother. Yeah, there weren't too many girls at school who he could flirt with—the fat kids with the pimples were usually the outcasts—but he could always find an audience with disaster.

Disaster, after all, was known to have many companions.

The buzzing was coming from right beside him now. With dawning horror, Danny noticed the wasp nest wedged snugly in the crook of a large limb. He'd never noticed it before, and he'd just climbed this tree last week. The size and shape of a football, it looked like it'd been punted there from some kid on the ground, and the tree caught it, nurtured it.

Danny's eyes grew large as he stared at the squirming mass of insects crawling out of the hole at the bottom of the nest. They surged ahead and took to wing, filling the air with their buzzing black shapes.

He was only about five feet away from the nest. Surely they'd sting him if he stood there gawking much longer, so he had to decide quickly: go up the rest of the way, where Ryan was waiting for him, or climb back down the tree, where Thomas and Emma would probably tease him for being a big, greasy coward.

A wasp landed on a leaf next to his hand. It swiveled its body to look at him with its tiny black eyes, its hind end twitching (What did Mr. Coleman, his science teacher, call that part of a bug's body? The addendum or something?). Then it leapt into the air again, did a funny twirling dance, and divebombed his hand. It landed stinger-first, and the pain that radiated from the wound made Danny howl in agony.

"What's wrong, bro?" Ryan called down.

"I got stung by a wasp!" Danny shouted back, sticking the burning wound in his mouth to soothe it. "There's a nest down here."

"Keep going," Ryan advised. "They can't all getcha."

"You're a funny guy, Ryan."

The cold hard truth of it was that he hated yellowjackets, hornets, paper wasps, all of them, since the age of five when he stepped on one in the backyard and it buried its needlelike stinger deep into his heel. His heel had turned purple, and the rest of his foot swelled like a balloon. Visions of amputation followed him to bed that night, where all he could imagine was himself hobbling around on one leg while his friends made pirate noises and called him IHOP and Lee Ning.

Eventually, his foot got better, but not before he vowed to never get stung again.

"Keep moving!" Ryan urged.

And so Danny moved. Quickly. Putting one hand in front of the other and hauling himself by whatever branch was within reach. The buzzing grew louder as the hive, no doubt notified by their scout that a fat kid with sweaty skin was in the vicinity, streamed out of the hive like a faucet and swarmed around Danny's head, neck and arms. They landed all over, sometimes stinging, sometimes just tickling his skin with their probing feet or flitting wings. He batted at them, bawling, as he kept climbing higher up the tree toward Ryan, whose eyes bulged with terror.

"Oh my God, dude, get away from me! They're all over you!"

Danny didn't hear him. He kept climbing, oblivious to everything but the searing pain racing up and down his body. Where was he going? He had no idea. To the top of the tree…to the clouds…to the top of the whole world! Anywhere where the air was sweet and cool, and the breeze would kiss his skin.

And where there'd be no wasps at all.

Below him, cutting through the buzz-saw din of manic insects, came the tinkling chimes of Amy Watson's voice. The girl from fifth-period English. The girl he'd had a crush on since the third grade. He'd invited her today to impress her with his tree climbing skills. And maybe steal a kiss from her afterward.

She was saying something to him, but he couldn't hear what it was. He stopped and looked down. His eyes stung with sweat and at first everything was a blur, and then Amy and his other friends came into focus. They were all screaming and pointing up at him. What were they saying to him? What did they—

Criiiiick-cruuunk. The branch he stood on snapped below his feet, and the tree itself seemed to lurch forward. Not by a strong wind, but by a force that emanated from within the trunk and seemed determined to knock him off.

He crashed through the tree, his face and gut slapped and punched by passing limbs, his neck and chest stabbed not once or twice but three times by sharp, stubby branches.

The world was a topsy-turvy complexity of colors. A whirling medley of sounds, ending abruptly with the shrieking siren of broken bones, as he came to rest on the lowermost limb of the tree. Draped like wet laundry, drip-drip-dripping on the roots snaking through the grass.

He could no longer hear the screams of his friends, or see Amy pass out and become the mental basket case that she was today. Or realize, as Ryan did as he hastily scooched down the tree, that the wasps—those fierce little assassins of the insect world—had vanished as quickly and mysteriously as they had appeared.

As if they had never been there at all.

A cold wind whipped their coats and flipped their hair in front of their faces as they gazed up at the tree.

"I remember now," Emma whispered.

"What do you remember, Emma?" Ryan pressed, moving to stand closer to her.

"The tree..."

"Tell us."

Emma glanced around, confused. "Well, didn't any of you see it, too? The tree *pushed* him."

"Yes," Julie agreed quickly. "It was like it wanted him to fall. The branch broke, and the whole thing kinda shifted to one side—"

Thomas stormed up to the tree and put his hands on the trunk, as if daring it to retaliate. "Trees don't *do* things like that. They're not alive; they don't *hurt* people."

"That's right," Elliot added, but quietly, with the least amount of conviction among the group.

"You saw it, too, didn't you, Elliot?" Ryan moved to stand in front of the much shorter man now, who wouldn't meet his eyes. "Tell us what you saw."

At first Elliot wouldn't reply, but then he raised his eyes to stare fiercely at Ryan. "You want to know what I saw that day? I saw *you*, Ryan, encourage Danny to keep going, even though he was freaking out. Everybody knew how much he hated bees. He was hurt, but you told him to keep going. Why did you do that? You could have tried to stop him, help him down. He was your best friend!"

"That's enough, Elliot," warned Thomas in a low voice. "He's suffered enough—we've *all* suffered enough. It's time to go home."

"Home?" Ryan spun around to face Thomas. "No one's leaving here."

"What are you talking about?"

Ryan yanked a gun out of his jacket pocket and leveled it at Thomas's head. Behind him, he heard Emma and Julie gasp.

"Where are you going now, Mr. Politician, huh? You gonna just walk away from all this like nothing happened and give a pretty speech?"

"Ryan, take it easy—"

"It's so easy for you, isn't it?" Ryan continued, switching the gun to the other hand. "You probably compartmentalized this a long time ago. You worthless politicians are good at that sort of thing. It's always someone else's fault, never your own."

"I didn't push him out of the tree."

"Ryan, please, listen to me." Emma slid up next to him and touched the arm with the gun. She tried to lower it, and he almost let her, but then his resolve hardened, and he shrugged her away.

"Don't touch me, Emma. You and Julie aren't any better. Neither of you even cried at his funeral."

"We all mourn in our own ways, Ryan."

Ryan turned his venomous gaze on Elliot. "Thanks for the pop psychology, Freud. I seem to recall you weren't even at the funeral at all."

"I was getting stoned." Elliot admitted, shame-faced. "I-I couldn't face what happened."

"No." Ryan looked around at his childhood friends like he was noticing them all for the first time. "None of you could."

"What are you going to do?" Julie asked in a small voice.

Ryan held up the revolver and cocked it. "With this? I don't know, maybe I should shoot you all dead right here."

Emma made a whimpering sound.

Ryan grinned. "But I'm not." He walked around the tree, once, twice, humming a little song to himself. The others recognized it at once as Radiohead's *Creep*. Danny listened to it over and over again when they were kids. He told Ryan and Thomas he was learning the words so he could serenade Amy with it when he asked her to the seventh-grade dance.

The words were still stuck in their heads after all these years. Julie started singing them softly to herself:

"When you were here before
Couldn't look you in the eye
You're just like an angel
Your skin makes me cry"

"Put the gun away, Ryan," Emma said, "and just tell us what you want!"

Ryan lowered the gun, pointed it to the ground. Slowly, he released the hammer. "I could never kill you, Emma." His eyes shimmered with tears. "Or any of you. At least not by choice."

He slipped the gun into his coat pocket. The others breathed an audible sigh of relief, though none dared to speak. "I must go now to be with Danny."

"What do you mean?" Julie asked.

"This is why you're all here, why I've asked you to come. For all these years I've returned to this place, alone, wracked with guilt. That day my friend's body hung here, lifeless, you all ran—but I stayed. I brought him down.

"And his eyes spoke to me that day. There was no fear in them. Only resolve. He wanted me dead. I can't go on living with the guilt and the nightmares any longer."

Ryan jumped and grabbed onto the lowest limb, hoisting himself up onto it into a sitting position.

"What are you going to do, Ryan?" Thomas's face turned pale.

"What do you think? I'm going to climb the tree."

"Don't—"

"And then I'm going to jump, Thomas."

Emma let out a soft cry.

"This is crazy, man," Elliot pleaded with him. "Come down and be with us. Let's get some drinks, sort it all out..."

"It's too late for that." Ryan stretched his arms and found another stout branch with which to pull himself up. "And if any of you cowards even think of running, remember—I have the gun."

"You think you're the only one who suffered?" Emma screamed up to him. "You think you're the only one who's had nightmares? I can't get the image of Danny out of my mind, either. I remember all the questions that were asked of us, and the scorn and blame placed on our shoulders. People didn't get it; they didn't see!"

Ryan didn't answer. He climbed the tree faster, with the expert precision he had as a kid.

Thomas paced back and forth. "You want to die so badly, why don't you just shoot yourself? You could've done it any time. Why do we need to see you die?"

At this Ryan stopped and looked down at the others. "We were in it together at the beginning; we'll be in it together at the end."

"Don't..." Emma sobbed.

Ryan was lost to them in the darkness of the tree. The sun had set, and the sky was salted with stars. The tree now looked like a giant black fist thrust into the air triumphantly, clutching Ryan somewhere in its leafy grasp.

Then they heard a sharp crack of wood. Ryan's startled cry echoed across the clearing as his body crashed through the leaves and branches, striking the ground at their feet with a sickening thud.

Ryan moaned and looked around him, blood pouring from his mouth and nose. He raised his arms helplessly, but they were broken, smashed like both of his legs. The others raced to help him and stop the bleeding. Julie tried to call for help on her cell, but slammed the phone down in frustration when she couldn't get through to anyone.

Ryan coughed a spray of blood, his eyes rolling up into the back of his head.

"Stay with us," Thomas begged. "Don't go, man. We want you alive."

Ryan focused blearily on Thomas and asked, "Why?"

Suddenly the wind dropped off, leaving them shrouded in silence. Then, faintly, a vibration started under their feet from deep within the ground. Next came the sounds of grinding, churning soil, and a crack opened up in the ground next to the trunk of the tree.

Emma screamed.

"Go, go, go!" Pushing her friends back down the hill. "Run!"

But they stayed.

The tip of a root squirmed out of the ground and slithered toward Ryan's leg, stopping at his knee to sip the sticky sweet blood pooling there. Then it lashed out with incredible speed and wrapped itself around his leg like a tourniquet, squeezing. Another leathery-looking root shot from the earth and spread across Ryan's chest, pinning him to the tree trunk.

They twisted, squeezed, and were soon joined by other blood-letting tentacles. The others watched hypnotically as the tip of one root slid into Ryan's mouth and wriggled down his throat. He gagged and choked until he finally closed his eyes for good.

Their thirst slaked, the roots recoiled into the depths from which they'd sprung, where they would now grow longer and stronger each year.

The tree trembled in the still air. Leaning forward ever so slightly, its branches closed in on the huddled group, who were too shocked to move or speak. In the rustling leaves above, a child's voice whispered:

"Climb with me, guys…"

And they climbed, one by one.

We're glad you enjoyed this book.
Read on for a sneak peek at *Curse of the Witch* by David R. Smith. Available on Amazon.

ONE NIGHT THE RAIN began to fall...

...and the old man knew his time had come.

Not through any magical spells or sorcery, boiling cauldrons or crystal balls. It was a feeling of something amiss, a signal from some strange and dark place. His name whispered over and over, by an evil as ancient as time itself.

Spikes of fear stabbed the old man's heart. He was certain who was calling his name, who was coming for him tonight. He knew the legends and was a part of them himself.

She had come back.

The one who cursed him long before he was even born.

The old man's fingers trembled as he closed the book he'd been browsing. A storm had kicked up out of nowhere, causing the power to fail. The slithery movements of shadows caught his eye, the way they climbed and leapt from wall to ceiling in his bedroom. Every corner of the room quivered with them. The notion of a bottomless pit filled with vipers came to mind.

Shuddering violently, he found he couldn't breathe. His tongue sat like a hard lump on the bottom of his cottony mouth. He clutched at his chest and muttered an incantation under his breath, all the while trying unsuccessfully to push back the rising tide of horror inside him.

He hadn't the power to combat this dark magic, at least not alone. He was a dead man for sure.

The storm howled outside his cabin with the fury of demons. It beat its fists against the groaning walls. It screamed through the eaves. Then, suddenly, he heard the explosive shattering of glass. Violent wind raced through the cabin, ransacking everything in its path.

The old man stood on shaky legs and peered out the window at the fitful night. A burst of lightning cracked the sky and deafening thunder followed. *There's something very wrong about this storm*, he thought. And about the darkness itself. Something so sinister it could only be one thing, a magic far blacker than any he'd encountered before. But what power could unleash such fearful enchantment?

He started sifting through his books, looking for a possible explanation, when a strange smell filled the cabin. A sickly sweetness that reminded him of dying roses and rotten fruit.

Then, a sound followed the scent, a noise much closer and more distinct than the whispering of his name. A noise that made his heart lurch painfully and his throat dry up. A scratching-chafing-scraping sound coming from inside his own house.

From the other side of the door, where things were moving.

The old man moved to the door quickly and locked it. Then, scanning the room, he searched for a way to leave a message for the others when they arrived. A message that would not be discovered by the things outside when they broke down the door and dragged him away kicking and screaming into the night.

A chorus of howls from inside his own cabin froze his blood.

Panicked, he returned to the small writing desk in the

corner where he'd been sitting and rifled through its drawers until he found a black pen. Then he hurried around the bed to the opposite wall. He removed a framed painting and set it on the bed face down. With shaky fingers, he started writing his secret message, a simple yet clever code for a certain child he had in mind, one who was exceptionally perceptive.

He hoped she'd get the message in time.

He hoped the *other* one wouldn't find it first because if the other one did, it would be all over. Not only would he be killed—a fate sure to be slow and painful—but a centuries-old pact would be broken. He'd have betrayed his ancestors' trust and unleashed a terrible and ancient evil upon the world.

From the door came the sounds of scratching, clawing, and cracking wood. Whatever was out there was only moments away from getting inside.

The old man finished his message and returned the painting to the wall. He dropped to his knees and closed his eyes.

He hoped it would be over soon.

CHAPTER ONE

"I DARE YOU TO jump," Ryan said, nudging his sister. "I don't want to swim all alone."

The glistening pool lay waiting for them to make their decision. Were they going to dive in or not? Ryan wanted his sister to do something other than sit by herself and read all day, but Abby was having none of it. She stood beside him like a statue, arms folded across her chest, her puckered face determined not to smile or have any fun at all.

She is so different, he thought for the millionth time. Beginning with the day she came home from the hospital, he knew she wasn't like normal babies. She didn't cry or fuss. She was content to lay in her crib and stare oddly at the ceiling. Sometimes a funny expression flickered across her scrunched little face. In those moments she would often make a gurgling sound, wave, and then grow silent again. Ryan often wondered what she saw up there.

As she grew, Abby spent more and more time alone. She learned to read by age three. She talked in riddles and loved solving puzzles. She even invented a written alphabet that looked like ancient runes, whose meaning she never shared with anyone.

But perhaps the strangest thing about Abby was her fascination with the supernatural.

"If you don't go in, I'll push you," he warned. He placed a hand on her back, applied a little pressure. "You don't need to worry. You'll float like a feather; you always do."

That was another strange quirk about his sister. Water rejected her. If she tried to swim under it, water pushed her back up like it didn't want anything to do with her. He'd never seen anyone so buoyant before.

"Suit yourself," he said with a big sigh. "I'm going in. The sun is scorching my back."

Ryan cannonballed into the water, enjoying himself despite the sour look his sister was giving him.

"Hey, I'll give you ten dollars if you join me," he said when he emerged, pretending to take money out of his pocket. "No, make it fifty. Fifty dollars, and all you have to do is jump in. I'll be right here to save you if you start drowning, which you won't. They didn't name me captain of the varsity swim team for nothing, you know!"

Abby shook her head slightly. You silly boy, her expression seemed to say. When will you ever learn?

Ryan couldn't figure out what made his ten-year-old sister tick. Their parents thought it was autism; however, the specialist they'd consulted said that although she had some of the characteristics of autism, she was simply Abigail Rebecca Martin, blond-haired, green-eyed, pale-skinned, a shade under five feet tall, and quirky.

Very quirky.

Who else eats the food on their plate in alphabetical order? Or organizes the books in their bedroom by the Dewey Decimal System? She even taught Ryan who Melvil Dewey was, a librarian who came up with the classification system back in 1876.

A light breeze rippled the pool's surface. Abby looked up with curious intensity at the golden sunlight pouring down from the sky.

Anyone else would have jumped at the chance to make fifty bucks. But not his sister. Although she was strange, he had to admit he enjoyed her company. Like most people who talked very little, Abby was a good listener.

But the truth was she did speak, occasionally, though she didn't believe in wasting words on meaningless chatter. Like a host of one of those creepy paranormal shows, Abby would suddenly show up in his bedroom and start telling him about an ancient civilization or a mythological creature. He hung on every word; he couldn't help it. The oddities that tumbled out of her mouth were both bizarre and fascinating.

When she was finished, she would simply turn away from him and walk out. She didn't care if he had questions. He called those quirky moments Abby Snapchats because he didn't know what else to call them. They were random and intriguing, and although he'd admit it only to himself, those moments made him feel connected to his sister. He knew his relationship with her was not like other people's, but he didn't care. He was fond of Abby and felt highly protective of her.

"Let me see if I have this straight," he teased as he climbed out of the pool and walked over to the diving board. "You put on your bathing suit for nothing?"

She shrugged. "Mom made me." The words, like her expression, were curiously distant and detached. The voice of someone waking from a dream.

"Well, suit yourself, Abs."

He drew in a deep breath through his nose. Then, tensing his legs, he sprang into the air, and sliced cleanly down through the water. His fingertips brushed along the smooth bottom of the pool. He kicked his strong swimmer's legs twice and glided through the cool water to the other side of the pool.

In that moment of bliss, he thought if there were such things as mermaids, he could swim with them forever. Of course, the only person he knew who believed in mermaids was Abby, who never met a superstition she didn't like.

When he surfaced, he shook the water out of his eyes and looked around.

Abby was gone.

In the few seconds he'd been underwater, she'd somehow managed to make her escape. He spied her in the screened-in back porch, legs tucked up under herself and a big fat book laying open in her lap.

Of course. What else would she be doing?

Okay, enough is enough, he thought. He was going to get her outside again one way or another, even if it meant tying a rope around her legs and dragging her kicking and screaming into the sunshine.

It was for her own good.

He toweled off and joined her on the porch. He couldn't see the cover of the book she was reading, but the title in the top margin read: A Supernatural History of the World.

"How can you sit there reading this depressing junk when it's a beautiful day outside?" he scolded her.

He waited for a response, but when all he got was the silent treatment, he decided it was time to take direct action.

"Abby," he said, flopping down on the couch next to her, "do you care that you're the only kid in the whole town not playing outside right now?"

"They should be reading, too."

The absurdity of her answer made him laugh. And he knew she wasn't kidding. Abby was happiest when she was indulging her brilliant yet baffling mind in arcane subjects. Like their father, a former social studies teacher-turned-author who wrote books on ancient legends and folktales, Abby had a fondness for history. Especially dark history. And most amazing of all, her mind was a vacuum for knowledge. Nothing that went in ever came out. A photographic memory, Dad called it. A real blessing.

Or a curse, Ryan thought, depending on which way you looked at it.

Watching the intensity with which Abby was reading the book, he couldn't help wondering what was haunting that mysterious mind of hers today.

"I'm not leaving until you put that stupid book down and come outside," he declared.

"You'll have a long wait," she replied, casually turning a page.

"Okay, then." He snatched the book from her hands before she could protest. "I'm out of ideas; I guess I'll just harass you."

Abby gave a little yip like a wounded puppy. "Give it back, Ryan!"

"Hey, you're my kid sister, right? I gotta know what you're reading." He flipped through the pages and stared at the old, grainy illustrations. Here was the portrait of a man who looked to be at least a hundred years old, scowling fiercely in a long white wig. On the opposite page was an artist's sketch of an old-fashioned courthouse. A sobbing woman stood before an angry crowd of onlookers. She looked desperate and terrified as the panel of judges pointed at her accusingly. Ryan started reading aloud the caption below the photograph.

"'In 1692, Sarah Good was charged with witchcraft and sentenced to death by hanging in Salem, Massachusetts. James Hathorne, one of the judges at her trial, later wrote in his personal diaries…'"

"'...that he felt regret for his role in the unjust murders of so many people,'" Abby interrupted. She recited the rest of the caption from memory: "'To this day, visitors to Salem hear screams in the middle of the night, and feel an unmistakable presence watching them. Are they imagining unseen spirits? Or are they experiencing the ghosts of Salem's haunted past?'"

Ryan gawped at his sister. It gave him a cold tingle whenever he witnessed Abby's amazing abilities. He couldn't seem to remember where he put his homework most of the time, and yet Abby could perfectly recite whole passages out of a book.

Without a word, he handed the book back to her and stood up.

"Okay, Abs, let's change the subject," he said, wringing his hands. "Wanna play Frisbee?"

"No."

"Ride bikes?"

"No."

"Why not?"

"It's going to rain," she said.

"What? There's not a cloud in the sky!"

"It's going to rain," she repeated flatly, keeping her attention on the book. Her lips moved slightly when she read, but she didn't utter a sound. He wondered if that was her trick to remembering all the words she read.

"I think you're crazy," he said.

"I'll exercise when I get to Uncle Silas's place tomorrow."

They were planning to spend a week with their mom's uncle in his cabin deep in the Adirondack mountains. They hadn't visited him in two years, and everybody, including Abby, was excited for the trip.

"Then what do you want to do instead now?" he asked.

She looked up at him. The answer was obvious.

"Fine." He was about to leave when an unusual anger welled up inside of him. He rarely felt anything but affection for his sister, but sometimes her inscrutable nature got under his skin.

"You know what your problem is?" he began. "You're missing out on life. Yeah, you're smart, but books can't make up for the excitement of living and having fun."

He started to pace now, like their father did when he was lecturing them.

"Life isn't in those books, you know. You should get out more, make some friends. You fill your head with too much weird stuff. That's what's wrong with you— you don't believe in anything real!"

Outside, the sun slipped behind a cloud like a magician pocketing a coin.

"Then you know what your problem is, Ryan?" she answered him, closing the book with a loud thump. "You don't believe in anything you can't see or touch. You have no faith."

He froze. Her words stabbed him like daggers, but they didn't stop him from asking the question that was really on his mind. "What's wrong with you today, Abs? You're acting funnier than usual, even for you."

"Nothing."

"You're lying."

Abby chewed her lower lip, a nervous habit. When she spoke again, her voice contained a faint tremor. "It isn't lying if you don't want to tell the truth," she said.

"You know, you'd make a great politician."

Abby didn't respond to that, and he didn't push her anymore. Instead, he left the patio and was on his way back to the pool when he felt a drop of water strike his forehead.

He looked up.

The blue sky and the sun were gone.

It was starting to rain.

CHAPTER TWO

THE AFTERNOON STORM wore on. Ryan sat in his bedroom, playing video games and watching the lightning crackle and spark in the distance. Their house sat on the top of a small hill. From his second-floor window he could see over the nearby rooftops and into the valley that lay beyond.

The rumbling storm clouds rose like a craggy mountain range on the horizon. Ryan thought of a powerful god, enraged at humanity, who was going to wipe out every man, woman and child. As he watched the storm front grind closer, he thought he heard muttered threats in the whooping wind. Warnings? A sign of danger to come?

That was crazy. Storms didn't warn people, and they didn't have voices. They weren't a sign of anything except a cloud full of electrical charges looking for something to zap.

He knew what he was doing, and he didn't like it. He was worrying too much about Abby. Again. He often wondered what it'd be like to have a normal sister. Someone who wasn't picked on all the time, pushed around in the hallways, called names. It was no wonder Abby took refuge in the school library every chance she got. Or so he heard from his friends' younger siblings, the kids he secretly paid off with Skittles and M&Ms to watch Abby at school.

When she had any free time at school, she could usually be found sitting among the stacks, looking at books with weird titles like, The Encyclopedia of Mythological Beasts, Haunted Heartland of America, or How to Create Your Own Magical Amulet.

Sure, it was cool to watch Harry Potter movies, but most kids he knew didn't study the stuff. Or spend all their free time reading about people burned at the stake or demons abducting young children in the middle of the night. In fact, he didn't know anyone else into paranormal stuff as much as Abby.

One day, his father asked Ryan to privately keep an eye on Abby, though he never fully explained what "keep an eye on" meant. He just assumed it meant to protect her from bullies. And so that's what he did the day he got into a fight on the bus with Joey Hollister, an eighth grader who kept calling his sister "Spook."

That name stung Abby deeply, though she wouldn't talk about it. She wouldn't talk to anyone, not even Ryan, for a week after that.

Could he really blame anyone for thinking Abby was spooky? No, but that didn't give them a right to tease her. He wasn't sorry for the fight, or for the detention he got from the principal. He was just doing what any big brother who cared about his little sister would do.

Feeling claustrophobic, he turned off his Xbox and left his bedroom. Spending too much time in his own head made him crazy.

On his way to join his family downstairs, he took a detour without even realizing it. He found he did this often, his legs operating on autopilot, carrying him to his parents' room.

He knocked on the door and got a mumbled response.

He winced, feeling terrible. He woke his mother up. She was probably taking one of her now infamous long naps. It quickly went from a quick lie down a few months ago to a full-blown marathon sleeping session every afternoon.

Of course, he didn't blame her; who could? She needed the rest. Her body was fighting cancer.

When the oncologist revealed it to their family six months ago, Ryan felt the bottom drop out of his world and a long black tunnel open up. The life of a teenager—friends, hanging out, studying for tests—suddenly felt like the least important thing in the world. But his mother had talked him out of this attitude very quickly. She promised him she could fight the cancer growing in her bones much more effectively if she knew her family was staying intact, both physically and emotionally. He promised through a sheen of tears that he'd keep going with his life and his studies, including sticking with basketball and the swim team.

For a while he managed it quite well, and then his mother took a turn for the worse. The chemotherapy wore her out, she lost her hair and her appetite, and some days she was too weak to lift her head up off the pillows. Then would come the good days. The "sunny ones," she would call it. On those days she was able to get up and even nibble a little food at the table with them, smile, listen to their stories about their days, and laugh. They almost seemed like a whole, intact family again on those days. Almost. But Ryan knew those days would never last, and the clouds would roll back in.

Ryan opened the door slowly and stuck his head inside the stuffy room. The blinds were drawn, and the heavily shadowed room had the damp smell of sweat and medicine. His mother turned her head to look at him. She smiled, lifting Ryan's spirits. He was afraid she'd be angry with him for waking her.

"Come in," she said, waving him forward. "I was just getting up…"

"You don't have to." He came around to her side of the bed and sat down. "I just wanted to …"

"What?" she asked when he hesitated. She stroked his cheek. Her hand felt cold and clammy, and Ryan squeezed it in his own.

"This trip we're taking tomorrow," he began. "We don't have to—I mean, I can stay here with you if you need me."

She smiled at him. "You've always been a thoughtful boy, and I love you for that. No, I want you to go. You deserve to go and have fun. I'll be all right, I promise. The sun is coming back tomorrow, I can feel it."

Ryan smiled back reflexively, but he was feeling anything but happy. He'd heard her say the sun was coming back now for the last two weeks, but still her condition seemed darker every day.

"Okay, Mom."

"Besides, who will watch out for your sister?" she added with a grin. "You're the only one she'll talk to most of the time. Or trust."

She was right, but lately he'd overheard Abby and his mother talking plenty of times behind the closed door. Once he lingered in the hall to hear what they were saying. He felt guilty eavesdropping on their private conversation, but Abby would never tell him what they talked about. He was curious what she might know about their mother's condition, what knowledge she might have about her future.

There I go again, thinking of Abby like she's a mind reader or fortune teller. But wasn't she? How else could he explain the things he'd seen her do?

"I'll keep her safe," Ryan promised.

"I know you will." She paused. "She looks up to you, you know."

He was taken aback.

"Don't look so surprised, Ryan. She knows you're her protector, but it won't be a job you'll have forever. Someday she's going to grow up to be …" Here she hesitated, choosing her words carefully. "To be someone who will light the world up."

Light the world up. Yes, he could see that. Someday.

He kissed his mother on the forehead and turned to leave. "Get some rest," he said.

"I will," she sighed, her eyelids fluttering shut.

Ryan watched her for a moment before easing out of the room. As he was about to close the door, he heard her speak again, and he froze.

"The magic is in the box," she murmured.

Ryan looked in on her again, but she was fast asleep. What did she mean? What box? Could she have been sleep-talking? Abby did that sometimes, mumbling incoherent things under her breath while she slept. Feeling uneasy, he closed her door and went downstairs.

MEET THE AUTHORS

DAVID R. SMITH is the author of over twenty books of fiction and non-fiction for children and adults. His work has been featured in numerous magazines and most recently in the anthology *It Calls from the Forest* by Eerie River Publishing. He lives in Livonia, NY. Visit his website at www.davidrsmithbooks.com

OLIVIA A. SMITH lives in Livonia, NY and attends Livonia Middle School. In no particular order, she loves writing, hanging out with her friends, soccer, and playing with her dogs. This is her first book.

Made in United States
North Haven, CT
20 March 2022